SHADOW
OF THE
PHOENIX

November 21 1847

WRITTEN BY

MARY JANE GRUETT

Blaize
Raine
Race

Happy Adventures in and out of books!

ORIGINAL ARTWORK

BY JENNA DETROYE

Mary Jane Gruett

2013

Psalm 46:1-3

PRINTED IN THE UNITED STATES OF AMERICA

First edition published 2011.

ISBN 978-0-9818974-5-5

ATTENTION SCHOOLS: Quantity discounts available on bulk purchases of this book for educational purposes.

For information, please contact:
Sheboygan County Historical Research Center
518 Water Street
Sheboygan Falls, WI 53085
Website: www.schrc.org
Phone: 920.467.4667
Email: schrc@att.net

Front Cover Image: Drawing of the *Phoenix* circa 1847.
Back Cover Images: Upper left– The family of Jan Hendrik and Wilhelmina TenDollen Wilterdink, both survivors of the *Phoenix* disaster.
Upper right: Winterswijk, Boekhandel Albrecht (Albert bookshop)
Lower left: Hendrik Jan and Gerritje Damkot Kooyers Esslinkpas. Hendrik Esslinkpas was a survivor of the *Phoenix* disaster.

Shadow of the Phoenix

Table of Contents

The Story of the Phoenix

The 1840s were a time of great immigration from western Europe to the United States. People left for many reasons. Some sought religious freedom. Others fled from military service. Still others left for financial gain and the ability to own their own land.

Those long and arduous trips across the Atlantic Ocean to freedom took as long as three months. Once an immigrant arrived in New York or Boston or Baltimore their journey continued up the Hudson River and west along the Erie Canal to Buffalo.

In Buffalo passengers boarded another ship for the 1,000-mile-long cruise through the Great Lakes to Wisconsin ports. One of these steamers on the Buffalo-to-Sheboygan run was the *Phoenix*.

The ship spent the past nine days fighting the fall gales of the lakes. Aboard were more than 300 passengers and crew, many immigrants from The Netherlands.

Shadow of the Phoenix

It had made the trip through the Great Lakes many times. But, two hours before dawn on November 21, 1847, when the *Phoenix* was just eight miles from its destination, it caught fire. When all was said and done, more than 250 people perished in the disaster.

The *Phoenix* ordeal is well-documented. The Sheboygan County Historical Research Center has detailed files. A number of great publications relate the story. Two of them are: *Phoenix, The Fateful Journey* by John Textor and *Out of the Phoenix* by Descendants of the Phoenix.

This historical novel by Mary Jane Gruett tells the story of a surviving child of the disaster in realistic terms of the era. Though difficult at times, Derk Van Vliet, a young lad from Winterswijk, Gelderland, The Netherlands, survives and begins a new life in America.

Part One
WINTERSWIJK, GELDERLAND,
THE NETHERLANDS

Map from **Wintersvijkse Pioniers in Amerika,** *Willem Wilterdink, 1990*

Chapter 1

The Domper   Early March, 1847

Derk looked across the aisle of the stately Dutch church at his friend, Pieter. Was Pieter ready to play their Sunday game of Gotch Ya – making faces at each other, trying to make the other laugh first?

The game had two rules. It had to be a laugh, not just a smile, but the laugh couldn't be out loud. And no points were earned if either set of parents noticed them and frowned. So far, so good. The boys hadn't been caught.

There was a third unspoken rule. Both knew if they did get caught, they could never play the game again. Their parents would watch them like an owl watches for a fat mouse on a winter's night.

The game had been going on for – Derk didn't know how long- two years at least, as long as the boys had been friends. They had started the game in Latin school, filling the time between completing their work and the next class. The schoolmaster, however, didn't take kindly to such nonsense, so they moved their game to church.

Church? Yes. Never mind that the two friends were to be thinking about the words they were singing and saying during the worship services. Never mind that their parents would expect them to contribute to the discussion of the sermon during the noon meal. Never mind that their parents, who were right there, were ready to quash their misconduct with a raised eyebrow, a silent promise of consequences later at home. These obstacles were simply a challenge to overcome.

Earlier that morning eleven-year-old Derk and his family had dodged the puddles as they walked to the village. "Pa, could I sit next to the aisle?" Derk asked. He wanted to be able to see Pieter's face without leaning forward and looking around his sister, Hannah. The more movements he made, Derk reasoned, the greater the chance of Pa noticing him and thinking he was up to something.

"No," Pa had said, "you're the oldest. You sit between your sister and brother like you always do."

Derk itched to kick at a half-frozen chunk of snow at Pa's answer, but he thought better of it. Jacobus, Derk's younger brother, had already walked into a puddle and slipped on some hidden ice; he was sitting through the service in wet clothes.

Squeezed between Hannah and Jacobus, and with the pastor's sermon just starting, Derk sighed and sat back. Pa, and Ma holding baby Martin, sat at the other end of the pew, listening to every word the pastor said.

Martin smiled and reached for Derk. Ma let him slide off her lap and the toddler stepped over Jacobus' feet. Derk picked him up, wrapped his arms around him, stole a glance across the aisle and caught Pieter's eye.

Was Pieter starting the game? As Derk watched, Pieter pulled his mouth into a long, narrow oval, rolled his tongue and pushed it through the oval. Derk smiled, then turned and pretended to listen to the sermon. Pieter would have to do better than that if he wanted to make Derk laugh.

It's been two weeks! Two weeks! Derk fumed as he trudged through the woods to the school in the village. Why did my parents think it was a good idea to leave the village church and worship at a neighbor's home?

He glanced over his shoulder and saw his dog following him at a distance. "Bello, go home. You can't go to school with me. Go home!" Derk waited until the dog turned around and trotted in the direction of the Van Vliet's cottage.

I wish I lived in the village like Pieter does, Derk thought. Then we could go fishing together every day, not just once in awhile. I hope he remembers to bring the fishing poles today. At least, I get to see him in school.

Derk brushed his straight, flaxen hair out of his eyes and reset his cap. Shifting his book bag higher on his shoulder, he broke into a run. Arriving late would mean less time with Pieter.

Derk's thoughts drifted to the time Pieter had rescued him from the classroom bully, Evert, and his thrashing fists. Pieter had punched Evert in the nose a few times, drawing blood. Now Evert didn't bother Derk except to call him names.

Those solid punches to Evert's nose became the glue that stuck Derk and Pieter together as best friends. They were like David and Jonathan, promising to be best friends forever.

What had Derk's mother said? A friend who helps you in time

of need is like a brother. That was Pieter; he was like a brother.

Pieter had asked, "Why doesn't Evert pick on someone his own size? He is so stupid, such a domper; I wonder why his parents send him to school."

"Maybe he goes to school to beat up smaller kids," Derk said.

"Could be. He hasn't learned anything, even though he's been in school for years. My sister knows more than he does, even though she doesn't go to school." Pieter paused. "Elizabeth hates it that girls can't go to Latin school, but you know what? She can read better than that domper, Evert."

Around the bend in the path Derk saw Pieter arriving on the far side of the schoolyard with the fishing poles. Some boys were playing tag behind the school.

"Pieter! Pieter!" Derk shouted and waved. They met at the edge of the yard. "What are we going to do today?"

Pieter smiled. "Today I'm planning to get even with Evert for tattling on me."

"You mean the time you put the mouse in his desk, the one with the insides hanging out? And the blood dried on his slate?"

"Remember how he looked?" Pieter bulged out his eyes, stretched his face long and narrow, then formed his mouth into an "O" as he imitated Evert. The boys chuckled.

"What's your plan?" Derk asked.

"You'll see, but I need some help. Will you help?"

"Sure. What are you going to do?"

"Take a look at this." Pieter held his jacket pocket open.

Derk saw a potato about the size of his fist. "A rotten potato? I've got lots of those at home. What're you going to do with it?"

"Looks solid, doesn't it, but it'll splatter all over when it hits something." Pieter smiled. "And it'll smell BAD."

"You can't throw it at him…he'll see you, and you'll be in more trouble."

"I know, I know," Pieter answered, impatience in his voice. "That's where I need you. You get the schoolmaster's attention…." He glanced around to see if anyone was listening. Seeing no one, he continued, "Ask him to explain something. You know…mathematics… Latin. While he's busy with you, I'll walk past the jackets on the back wall and slip the potato into Evert's pocket. When we go outside for recess, I'll make sure he falls and smashes it…maybe trip him."

The schoolmaster stood at the door, ringing the bell. The boys picked up their book bags. This is a great idea, Derk thought, as they raced toward the building. I can't wait to see the face Evert will make this time.

+ + + + +

The schoolmaster dismissed the class for recess and the boys put on their jackets. A brisk March wind was blowing. Derk and Pieter, along with the other boys, followed Evert outside.

"Watch me," Evert said, standing at the edge of the porch. "I'm going to jump." He turned to face the boys behind him. "I dare you all to jump off after me. You, too, puny Derk, and all the rest. If you don't jump, you're a stinking, rotten potato!"

Evert turned back toward the edge of the porch. As he did so, he caught the point of one wooden shoe behind the other. Pitching forward, he fell, screaming, to the muddy ground.

The boys ran down the steps to help him. Evert got up slowly, brushing at the mix of mud and dried grass on his jacket.

"Are you all right?"

Evert nodded. A rotten potato smell spread through the air.

Derk and Pieter, stifling their laughter, ran behind the schoolhouse and hid in a clump of bushes.

"This is better than what I hoped for," Pieter said, in a loud whisper.

"Shh!" Derk put his finger to his lips. "The schoolmaster." He pointed to the window above them. "We don't want him to hear us.'

"Yeah," Pieter said in a low whisper. "Wasn't that great! The domper tripped himself!"

"And just who is that stinking, rotten potato that Evert was talking about?" Derk asked. "Must be him, the domper. He didn't jump off. He fell off!"

+ + + + +

After school Derk and Pieter shouldered the fishing poles, picked up the worms they had dug, and walked toward the canal.

"Hey, I sure missed you at church yesterday," Pieter said, "and last Sunday too...no one to make faces at me. You won last time at

Gotch Ya, but just wait, I'll win next time."

"Maybe there won't be a next time."

"What? Why do you say that?"

"Parents." Derk rolled his eyes. "They are making me go with them to our neighbor's house for worship services. Did I tell you what happened yesterday? It was terrible."

"What happened?"

"A crowd gathered outside the cottage and someone threw a rock through the window. Then an officer broke down the door. He said we all had to go home or we'd go to jail."

"Broke the door down? Did anyone get hurt?"

"No, but the rock missed the pastor by inches."

"Who was so mad they'd throw a rock? It could have hit someone! Why did they do that?"

Derk kicked at a pebble on the path and sent it flying into the ditch. "Pa says it's because we left the village church."

"Why did your parents leave the church?"

"Oh, I don't know. They say King William is telling the church what to do...and how to worship. Lots of stuff has changed. At least, that's what my parents say."

They reached the canal, threw down the fishing poles and took out the worms. Derk baited one for Pieter, then one for himself. "I don't like going to this house for church, but I have to do what my parents say."

Pieter tossed his line into the water and sat down. "Wait until we go to the university. Then we'll do what we want. That's what I'm waiting for."

"Going to the university together…that's going to be fun!" Derk threw his line in and sat down. "Do you know what you want to study? How about being a doctor like me?"

"I don't know about that…think I'd rather be a lawyer…or a professor. Being a doctor is kind of messy, isn't it? I don't even like to put a worm on a hook."

Derk smiled. That was true.

"Hey, I've got a bite." Pieter brought in a fish, took it off the hook, and put it into the pail.

Derk baited the hook for Pieter. "Being a doctor is messy? Maybe. My uncle's a doctor. Ma says he saved my life when I was a baby. I may be small and puny, but I'm here. I want to be a doctor so I can help people get well."

"I guess that's a good reason." Pieter jerked his line out of the water, then threw it farther out. "That's so unbelievable – throwing a rock through a window. Lucky no one was hurt. Did you know anyone in the crowd?"

"Some were from the church in the village. Others I didn't know." Derk shrugged his shoulders. "What made me mad was they called us dompers… like we don't know anything… like we're trying to be stupid…and stay stupid."

"You're going to Latin school," Pieter said. "You can't stay stupid in Latin school…unless you're Evert."

Derk laughed. "Yes, unless you're Evert, the domper."

Chapter 2

The Enemy   Mid-March, 1847

"Derk, please lower the food safe," Ma said. "We need cheese and bread for supper. How was school today?"

The boy unfastened the rope from the hook on the wall and lowered a metal box to the table. "Can we have some sausage, too?" he asked, as he removed a chunk of cheese and a loaf of bread from the safe.

"No, that's for Sunday."

Derk closed the box, pulled on the rope and raised it to the rafters again, out of the reach of vermin. "Ah, not much happened. It was a quiet day." He fastened the rope to the hook on the wall.

"Ma, that sickness I had as a baby…is that why folks say I'm puny?"

"Probably. I pray daily that you'll grow up as strong and tall as your pa." She turned toward the fireplace. "Oh, the fire's dying out. Add some peat, Derk."

He threw some turf on the smoldering fire. The smell of the burning peat spread throughout the room, giving some relief from the smell of rotting potatoes that permeated the air. He took out his pocket knife, picked up a small block of wood from the fireplace mantel and sat down to work on the owl he was carving.

"Ma, can someone be your friend one day and the next day be your enemy?"

"What do you mean, Son? Did something happen at school?"

"No, nothing happened at school. I mean, how can people change their minds so quickly? Some of those people calling us dompers last Sunday go to the village church." Derk held the owl up into the sunlight streaming in the window and inspected his work carefully. "They were our friends when we went to that church. Now they're throwing rocks at us." He rubbed his hand over the wing's surface, found a rough spot and smoothed it out with a few strokes of the knife.

"Lots of things can cause people to change their minds," Ma said. "Maybe something or someone got them riled up. Maybe the church leaders think if they punish us, others will be afraid to leave the church." She bent over the kettle hanging in the fireplace and stirred the soup. "Needs some salt."

"I just don't understand it," Derk said, pulling the blade across the wood. "How can people be so fickle?"

"Maybe those who are against us think they're being patriotic, being loyal to King William." She paused. "Maybe they think we're being unpatriotic. And sometimes people will do what they think they have to do – to get ahead, or to save their own skin."

On the far side of the room, Martin moved, waking from his nap. He sat up. Ma smiled at him. "You woke up just in time for supper, Martin. Tell the others that we're ready to eat, Derk."

+ + + + +

"Don't be so slow, Son," Pa called. "We don't want to be late for worship."

Derk ran to catch up with Pa and Mr. Schutt who lived on the next farm. Martin sat on Pa's shoulders and Jacobus walked at his side.

I wish I were taller, Derk thought, so I could reach up and tickle Martin in the ribs. He curled and uncurled his fingers as though he were touching Martin's ribs. "I'm going to tickle you, Martin."

The toddler giggled and kicked his feet against Pa's chest.

"How could the church leaders let the king take control of the church?" Mr. Schutt asked. "That was so wrong."

"I don't know," Pa said, shaking his head. "But I know this about the king; he does what he wants to do and no one can stop him."

"The king should be finding ways to reduce taxes, rather than trying to run the church." Mr. Schutt's voice rose in anger. "He should be trying to stop the potato blight, so we don't starve!"

"Uh, potatoes! I hope this year's crop will be better." Pa set Martin on the ground.

The toddler ran to Derk and took his hand.

"We need religious freedom," Mr. Schutt said, "like in A-mer-i -ka, across the ocean. A-mer-i-ka, I think that's how you say it. Some say they have religious freedom there."

"That doesn't help us," Pa said with a short laugh. "Guess we'll have to make the best of it here."

Ma, Hannah, and Mrs. Schutt caught up with them as they neared the cottage of Mr. and Mrs. Kees. Boards covered the window that had been broken the previous Sunday.

When they entered the house Mr. Kees said, "Our pastor was arrested yesterday. He's in jail and they want us to pay a fine to get him out. They charged him with preaching and holding church services… said he didn't have a permit."

After the men discussed how to raise money to pay the fine, the group sat down. Mr. Schutt led the psalm-singing. "The Lord is my shepherd, I shall not want…."

Pa stood up to read the sermon the pastor had prepared. "We must forgive our enemies," he began.

Derk tried to listen as Pa read the long sermon. Hunting rabbits in the woods with Bello was more fun, more exciting, than sitting on a three-legged stool and listening to a sermon.

Crash! Bump! Bump! Bump! Thud!

Derk, startled, teetered on the edge of the small stool. The thumping noise had come from above his head. He glanced at the ceiling of the cottage.

The food safe swung back and forth like a pendulum. Derk half expected the box to break loose from its hook and spill its contents on the worshipers. A slight smile crept across his face as he thought of how Mrs. Kees would look with some slices of bread atop her white lace headdress.

A second crash was followed by a bump, bump, bump, thud. Again the food safe swung. Derk crouched on the stool, preparing for another rock to come through the window.

"Dompers, dompers!"

"Open up, open up, you Seceders," someone shouted, pounding on the door.

A baby began to cry and other small children joined in.

Derk froze. He knew someone would be arrested today. He felt sick, sick enough to lose his breakfast in front of everyone.

Pa walked to the door and opened it.

An officer stepped into the room, while a second officer stood outside. "Where's your permit?" He shouted to be heard above the cries of the children. "You need a permit to hold this meeting! Where is it?"

Pa asked for silence. He looked around the room and the cries gradually hushed to sobs. "We don't need a permit, do we?" He spoke with respect. "The prohibition against meeting together was revoked by King William a few years ago."

"Yes, but for a church service you need the king's permission. Civic meetings are exempt, but worship services aren't."

The officer took a step toward the door, then turned and faced the group. "You don't have a permit. Who's in charge and who owns this house?"

Mr. Kees and another man rose slowly, then went and stood next to Pa.

"You three are under arrest. Step outside, now."

There were twice as many people outside as last week, including some older children. Derk scanned the new faces. He didn't know most of them. Then he saw Pieter's pa and standing next to him... Pieter! Why was he there? Pieter held something in his hand and a scowl framed his face.

As the officer bound his hands, Pa looked at Derk. "Take care of Ma, the little ones, and the farm, Son."

The others watched as the officers led the three men away.

Derk started for home beside Ma, walking straight, trying to look taller. He tried to ignore the queasy feeling in his stomach. Take care of Ma, he said to himself. Take care of the younger children. Do Pa's chores. Milk the goats. Take the extra milk to the cheese maker. Feed the pig. Dig up the ground to plant the rye. School! His shoulders slumped. There'd be no time for school. He'd have to drop out!

Something whizzed past Derk's ear. It hit a fence post and splattered. A rotten potato. It had been meant for Derk and he knew who had thrown it: Pieter, his old friend, his new enemy.

Chapter 3

Potato Wars April, 1847

Derk held his nose, trying to block out the smell of the potatoes he carried in a basket. Bello trotted beside him.

No escaping the odor, Derk thought as he skirted the puddles on the path to the barn. It's in the house, yard, fields, village, woods... all over.

The smell reminded him of the carcass of a dead squirrel he found in the woods. That smell was bad...but you could walk away from it. No one in Winterswyk could walk away from the rotten potato smell.

When he reached the barn he picked out some potatoes that looked solid and placed them on a shelf above the goat's pen. He wanted potatoes that wouldn't turn to mush in his hand when he used them for target practice. Walking down the lane with Bello at his heels, Derk would pick out a fencepost, size it up and take aim. "Take that, Pieter," he'd say when the potato splattered.

He laughed when he thought about how Pieter's clothes would stink. Whew! Just like Evert's stinking jacket. The smell had been so bad that the schoolmaster had sent him home.

Derk dumped the remaining potatoes into the pig's trough, then turned away as they split open. Rooting through the mess, the pig found breakfast.

"Sum, es, est; sumus, estis, sunt." Derk reviewed Latin verbs as he picked up the bucket. He sat on the stool and put his forehead against the goat's warm side. Streams of milk pinged as they hit the bottom of the pail. "Sum — I am. Es — you are...."

Last spring Derk had helped Pa plant the potatoes. When they came up, the plants looked strong and healthy, but by early summer, dark spots appeared on the leaves. Many of the potatoes were rotten when they dug them in fall. The neighbors' crops were bad, too. I hope Pa's right, Derk thought. I hope the crop will be better this year.

He whistled for Bello. "Buckets are full, Bello. Let's go."

Jacobus held the door open for Derk as he carried the buckets inside the cottage.

"Two full buckets today," Ma said, as Derk set them on the floor. "Good."

Derk walked to the fireplace where Martin sat on a stool, bare-footed. "Where are your socks, Martin?"

The toddler shrugged his shoulders. "Don't know." Derk grabbed Martin's feet with his cold hands. Martin cried out and jerked his feet away.

"Derk! Don't tease," Ma scolded. "He could fall into the fire. Hannah, help Martin put his socks on. We can't have him getting sick, on top of our other troubles."

Hannah put her knitting on the mantel. "Come on, Martin. We'll put your socks on,"

As Derk warmed his hands at the dying fire, he thought about the edge in Ma's voice. She has a lot to be nervous about – Pa being away for so long, no turf to burn and no money to buy flour.

The pulley on the food safe squeaked as Jacobus pulled on the rope. "Listen to this," Jacobus said, raising and lowering the safe. "It squeaks like a mouse."

"Jacobus, don't play with that!" Ma chided. "Pull the rope so the safe is up high and fasten it to the hook. What if it would break? Your pa's not here to fix it. We don't want rats to get into our food."

Ma cut slices of dark bread and put a piece in each bowl. "Derk, you and Jacobus must gather some fallen branches in the woods this afternoon." She dipped milk from one of the buckets and poured it over the bread in the bowls.

They stood around the table. Ma asked the blessing and then they all sat down on their stools.

Derk tried to ignore the smell of the bread as he choked it down. Ma, trying to make their food supply last another day, must have added some potatoes to the bread, he thought. He washed it down with the milk.

"Today you can sell the extra milk and buy some flour, so I can bake bread," Ma said. "Derk and Hannah, get ready. You'll carry the milk to the cheese maker."

"I can do it myself," Derk said. "I'll use the yoke that Pa uses." He took the yoke from its hook on the wall and said, "Pieter carries water with the shoulder yoke. If he can do it, I can do it." He put his jacket on and placed the yoke across his shoulders.

"Don't compare yourself to Pieter," Ma said. "He's older than you."

24

Derk frowned. He may be older, but I can throw better and I can outrun him any day, he said to himself.

He stooped to hook the bucket handles onto the yoke. Slowly he straightened up and felt the heavy weight on his shoulders. He took a step forward and the milk sloshed around and over the edges and onto the floor. Frowning again, he lowered the buckets, unhooked them, and hung the yoke back on the wall.

Ma sighed and picked up a bucket. "Let Hannah help you. Bring the pole and let's go outside. You'll have to walk to the village twice today, carrying one bucket now and one later." She carried the milk outside.

"Derk, you go in front," Ma said.

He put the pole on his shoulder and gripped the pole with his hand. Hannah took the other end and put it on her shoulder.

Hooking the bucket on the pole, Ma said, "Walk carefully and don't spill it. Look for firewood on the way back. Here's some bread for lunch." She slipped two pieces of bread into Derk's pocket.

As the bucket swung between them, they started toward the village. Bello bounded along, scaring a rabbit into its hole.

Hannah sang as they walked along. Now and then Derk pointed out some fallen branches. When Hannah stopped between verses, Derk said, "I wish Pa and Ma hadn't left our old church…then Pa wouldn't be in jail. It's hard on Ma when Pa's gone. Did you hear it in her voice? She's worried."

"I don't like it when she's worried," Hannah said. "I pray every night that Pa will come home soon."

"What's the use of praying?" Derk asked. "God isn't answering."

"Not yet, but I know He will." She began singing again.

Birds called to each other and Bello barked as she chased a saucy squirrel up a tree. I wish I were in school, Derk said to himself. I wonder what they're studying in mathematics. Will I ever get a diploma so I can go to the university?

They were nearing the village. The cheese maker lived on the far side of town, and they would have to pass the school. Suddenly Derk realized that the school was just around the next bend in the path. "Stop singing, Hannah," he said, his voice terse. She stopped walking.

"Ahhh," Derk cried, as the milk sloshed over the brim of the bucket and into his wooden shoe. "Don't stop without telling me. Look what you've done – spilled some milk."

"Sorry. Why should I stop singing?"

"Just be quiet," he said through clenched teeth. "Just be quiet. Now let's start again. Are you ready?"

"Oh, you don't want your friends to see that you need help from a girl."

Her words cut to his heart. She's just like Evert, making fun of my size. She was right, but he wouldn't tell her that. As they passed the school, Derk saw the playground was clear. He breathed a sigh of relief.

The cheese maker gave them a few coins for the milk. They took the money to the miller next door and he filled the bucket with rye flour.

"I'm tired," Hannah said, sitting down on the miller's doorstep. "Let's sit here and eat our bread."

"I'm not tired. I could carry buckets all day, but if you want to rest, we'll rest." Placing the pole and bucket on the grass, he took the bread from his pocket and handed a piece to his sister.

Down the street a door opened and a girl about Derk's age came out. It was Pieter's sister, Elizabeth, with a basket on her arm. She walked toward them. "Hello, Hannah."

"Hello, Elizabeth," Hannah said. "Where are you going?"

Elizabeth stopped. "I'm taking lunch to my pa at the shop. Why did you come to the village today?"

"We carried the milk to the cheese maker," Hannah said. "Our pa usually does it, but he...he couldn't today."

Bello stood up and sniffed Elizabeth's hand. She rubbed the dog's head. "Good dog, Bello," she said.

"I think Bello likes you," Hannah said.

"I think so, too," Derk said. "Bello doesn't like everyone."

Elizabeth smiled. "I wish I had a dog like Bello," she said. "Pa says I can have a dog someday. I have to go now. My ma can't be alone for too long. 'Bye." She turned and walked down the street.

Derk drew in his breath. Lunchtime. Pieter would be coming home from school! The last of the bread stuck in his throat as he heard a familiar whistle.

Pieter stopped at the door of his house. "Hey, Domper Derk. You can't carry that milk by yourself? A girl has to help you? You're

27

not only puny, you're a weakling and a domper, Domper Derk!" He stepped inside and closed the door.

Picking up the bucket of flour, Derk said, "Let's go! You carry the pole."

"I'm not finished with my bread."

"I'm going! Pick up that pole!"

Hannah stuffed the bread into her mouth and picked up the pole. Derk started off at a fast pace, and Hannah ran after him, dragging the pole behind her.

Before he left for the cheese maker with the second bucket of milk that day, Derk went to the barn. He picked the biggest potato off the shelf and put it carefully into his pocket.

This time he carried the bucket alone. Whenever one arm got tired, he switched the bucket to the other one. The cheese maker paid him and he started home.

The streets were empty as Derk neared the school. He walked into the woods beyond and hid the bucket under a bush. Then he crept quietly back toward the school and hid in some bushes under the open window.

From this position he could hear the boys reciting their Latin lesson, words unfamiliar to Derk's ears. He had missed so much in a month.

He wondered if he'd ever be able to get caught up, then felt anger rising within him. If his parents hadn't left the village church, his pa wouldn't be in jail. And he'd be in school, completing the year's work.

He was no closer to a diploma now than he was a year ago. Pieter would be in the university soon and Derk would still be in Latin school. He shook his head in disbelief. How had things changed so quickly?

The schoolmaster's sharp tone of voice brought Derk up short. Pieter would be staying after school for talking back to the teacher. This was perfect.

The master dismissed the pupils. All his classmates came out, except Pieter. After they left the schoolyard, Derk shifted his position and got more comfortable.

No one was in sight when the door opened again. This time Pieter came out, alone.

Derk waited until Pieter walked past the bushes and a distance beyond. Then he stood up, drew back his arm, and let the potato fly. By the time Pieter knew what hit had him, Derk was running home through the woods.

Chapter 4

Amerika Fever   *June 1847*

"Come, Derk," Pa said. "Let's look at those potatoes."

Bello trotted along as they started for the potato field in the far-thest corner of the farm. Derk found a stick and threw it. "Fetch, Bello," he called. Bello brought it back and Derk threw it again.

The boy ambled along behind Pa, whistling. A few days ago his pa and the others had been released from jail. It seemed unlikely that any in the group would again be arrested for holding worship services in a home. Now they held services on a barge.

The barge, owned by the pastor's brother, was docked in a nearby canal. For the past few weeks, the Seceders had boarded the ca-nal boat for worship. The king's officers could do nothing but watch.

It's wonderful to have Pa home and all of us together again, Derk thought. I'm happy Pa wants to see how the potatoes are growing. He took a deep breath, enjoying the morning sunshine.

Derk was proud of his work in the potato field. After Hannah and Jacobus had helped him plant the potatoes, Derk took over all the care. He hoed every inch of the field and got all the weeds out. Later he hilled each plant, bringing the ground up around each stem.

He dropped a few more paces behind Pa and shielded his eyes to look for Bello. Seeing her near the field of rye grain, he ran to catch up with Pa's long strides. "I can go back to school next term, can't I? I studied my notes every day."

"I think so." Pa said, stroking his beard. "I know how much going to school means to you."

Derk smiled, happy that his pa understood. Pa had wanted to be a doctor, too, but his education was cut short after Latin school. When grandfather had become ill with cholera, Pa had to stay home and do the farm work, supporting his two brothers who were studying at the university. Uncle Johannes was a professor now and Uncle Willem was a doctor in Leyden, but Pa, as he put it, was "a poor farmer on rented land."

Bello's barking brought Derk back to the present. She raced toward them.

Standing at the field's edge, Pa gave a long, low whistle as he looked at the new crop. "Looks good, Son; the rows are straight and even. You have used the hoe well." Derk could hear the pride in his voice.

Pa walked into the field and down the long rows. Derk followed with Bello at his heels. Thump! Pa stopped abruptly and knelt down. Derk bumped into him and Bello's legs got tangled up with Derk's. Boy and dog hit the ground, crushing some potato plants.

"Bello," Derk scolded, as he got up. He brushed off the soil that clung to his breeches. Turning back to Pa, he asked, "Is something wrong?"

Pa's lips formed a tight line as he stood up and stepped into the next row. There he knelt again.

Derk stepped next to him. Pa walked farther into the field, stopping to look at plants here and there.

"Lord, have mercy," Pa said in a whisper.

"What's wrong?" Derk studied his face.

Pa picked a leaf and handed it to him. It had tiny brown and black spots. "Roll the leaf between your hands."

Derk mashed the leaf between his palms, then put it up to his nose. It was the same smell that came from the potatoes he fed to the pig every day.

+ + + + +

A few weeks later Derk was awakened by the low voices of his parents. He lay quietly, not wanting to disturb Jacobus.

"How can we leave?" Ma said. "This is our home."

"How can we stay? The potato crop has gone bad. We struggled last year to pay rent and taxes, Everything is taxed, even flour."

Pa's voice got louder. "And now there's a tax on butchering your own animals. Last week Schutt slaughtered his hog. The next day the official was there, knocking on his door, demanding that he pay a tax for butchering his own hog!"

"Shhh. The children."

"I'm sorry. I get so angry at the government. All it does is take our money. We can never save up enough to buy our own land."

No one spoke for a long time, then Pa's voice broke the silence. "Jan Arend's letter said there are no such taxes in Amerika."

Amerika! Derk clamped his hand over his mouth to cover a gasp.

"Please read the letter again," Ma said.

Derk held his breath as Pa read.

"It was difficult for me to leave, but I never wish to go back. There are just as many poor people here as rich individuals. No one here has to doff his hat for anyone. The rich respect us because we work for them. We have freedom to worship and there are many of God's people here; we have joined them. Come for the sake of the children."

Pa cleared his throat and paused before speaking, "I want my children to get a good education. Derk should have the chance I didn't have."

"Derk is so much like you," Ma said. "He spent every free moment with his studies…reviewing Latin, doing mathematics." She sighed. "I missed you so much. I'm so glad you were here for moving day in March. That would have been awful without you."

Derk silently agreed with Ma. Packing all their belongings on a cart and moving to another tenant farm every March first was awful enough. The land owner always made sure Pa and the laziest tenant switched farmsteads; the owner knew that Pa would repair the buildings and do his best to build up the soil so the crops would grow well the next year.

"The once–a–year move – another crazy law. If you're renting a farm, why should you move to a different farm after a year? It makes no sense to rotate the crops and make improvements so you can get ahead. Someone else profits from your hard work the next year!"

"Yes," Ma said, "it's a way to keep poor tenants poor."

Derk breathed slowly and softly.

"How will we get money to buy passage on a ship?" Ma broke the stillness with her question.

"We can sell the grain from the field. That will give us enough money to buy traveling in steerage on the ship. We can take as many goods as we want because baggage goes free."

Silence.

"Others from the village are planning to go after the grain harvest," Pa said. "We could join them. Selling the goat will bring extra money for the trip."

"I don't know." Ma sighed again. "How can we leave our friends? We'll never see them again!"

"Come, let's go to bed. We have time to think about this."

Have I been dreaming, Derk wondered, long after it was quiet.

What Pa said was true. Many families had gone to Amerika. Some from Winterswyk had left last month.

He lay back on the pillow and listened to Jacobus' even breathing. Are there schools in Amerika? The letter had said nothing about school. How could he complete Latin school, get into the university and study to be a doctor if he were in Amerika?

Maybe God could work a miracle and change things so they could stay in Holland, but would He? "God," he prayed, "I can't go to Amerika, I'll never get to be a doctor. Keep us here in Winterswyk. Amen."

Pa said he would sell the goat. What about Bello? Did that

mean Bello couldn't go to Amerika? Surely not! Derk couldn't leave his dog Bello behind. Bello, who had helped him get the pig back into its rickety pen again and again, who kept him company in the potato field, the only one who stuck by him…his only friend.

Leave Bello behind? He couldn't do it!

He turned toward the wall with tears streaming down his face.

Chapter 5

The King's Edict   August 1847

Daylight shone in the window as Derk bounded out of bed. The bright Sunday morning was marred only by the smell of potatoes rotting in the fields.

"Martin, eat your bread," Ma said, as Derk joined his family for breakfast.

"You want to go on the boat today, don't you, Martin?" Derk asked.

Martin smiled. "Boat!" He took a big bite.

+ + + + +

With Martin riding piggyback, Derk walked ahead toward the

canal. He was followed by his family and their neighbors, the Schutts. Mrs. Schutt carried their new baby. Other families joined them as they walked along.

"Down," Martin said.

Derk stopped, squatted and Martin slid off his back. He took Martin's hand and they walked on.

After rounding the bend in the road, Martin stopped and pointed. "Boat," he said, hopping up and down.

Derk knelt to be eye level with the toddler. "Shall you and I go on the boat?"

"Yes!"

A number of families were gathered on the shore, ready to board the barge.

Martin tugged at Derk's hand. "Go on the boat," he said, pointing.

"Let's wait for Pa and Ma," Derk said. Looking back, he saw his family rounding the bend. He took Martin's hand and they walked slowly toward the barge.

Derk stopped. "What's that sound?" He cocked his head, straining to listen. Hoofbeats. "Listen, Martin, A horse is coming. Do you hear it? It's coming fast."

The horse appeared around the bend, coming straight at them. The rider made no attempt to slow the horse.

Ma screamed, "Get Martin!"

Derk grabbed his little brother under the arms, swung him off the path and onto the grass near the trees, just in time to escape the flying hoofs. Martin clung to Derk, terrified.

The official reined in the horse where Derk and Martin had stood moments before. "I represent His Majesty, King William," the officer said in a loud voice. He waited.

The pastor removed his cap and the other men followed his example. Derk put Martin down and reached for his cap. He bowed with the rest of the group.

"I bring word from the King to you Seceders." He spat out the last word and pulled a scroll from inside his shirt. Unrolling it, he held it up. Sunlight glinted off the gold seal. "This edict forbids worship on any boat, ship, or barge! You will be arrested, fined and jailed if you go on that barge!"

The group stood silent as the meaning of the words sunk into their consciousness.

Arrested, fined, jailed! The words scrambled themselves around in Derk's head. Jailed, arrested, fined! Fined, arrested, jailed! Not Pa! Not again!

"Don't stand there," the official barked. "Go home! Go home, you...you Dompers!" The horse whinnied.

Those on the barge stood quietly, stunned. Then a low rumble sounded through the group. The pastor shook his head in disapproval.

"You can't stay here," the official shouted, looking around the group. "You'll be arrested for an illegal gathering. Leave! Leave!" He waved his hands, shooing them away like they were chickens in a farm-yard.

Pulling on the reins he turned the horse around. Taking one more look at them, he muttered, "Dompers!" Then slapping the horse's rump, he galloped away.

A man stepped back on to the path and shook his fist at the disappearing official. "That dirty, rotten, low-down skunk of a king! How can he do this to us?"

"Never mind the king," another man said. "He puts on his shoes one at a time, just like everyone else."

A ripple of laughter came from the group, but quickly faded.

"We must respect those in authority over us," the pastor reminded them.

"How can we live under this unjust government?" Mr. Schutt asked. "We should leave this country!"

The pastor raised his hand for silence. "Brothers...." His voice sounded weary. "Brothers, go home and read God's Word. Pray with your family. Ask God for strength and guidance."

"Come, children!" Pa said. His eyes were blazing with anger.

Derk bent down and helped Martin crawl up on his back for the ride home.

At home, the family gathered around the table. Pa opened the Bible and read from the Psalms. "Lord, you have been our dwelling place in all generations."

He looked around the table, his eyes resting on each child for a moment. "Your Ma and I feel that we must be able to worship God with those who believe as we do. We have been praying about what we should do. We've been thinking about going to Amerika, as others have done."

Derk, looking across the table at Hannah and Jacobus, saw surprise on their faces. Pa looked at each child again. "That barge was our last hope of a place to worship, but the king's edict took that away. The king has driven us from our country."

He stroked his beard. "Some from our village are going to Amerika in a few weeks…and we'll join them. Starting tomorrow, Derk, you'll help me harvest the grain. Jacobus, you'll gather wood so Ma can bake bread and make cheese for the journey. Hannah, I'm counting on you to help your ma with whatever she needs. We have much to do before we go."

"Let's start right now," Jacobus said.

Pa shook his head. "Sunday is a day of rest, Son. We'll start tomorrow."

Later Pa went outside and Derk followed him. Bello sprang up from her place by the door, wagging her tail. Derk picked up a stick and threw it down the lane. "Fetch, Bello."

The dog bounded away, got the stick and brought it to Derk. He took it from her mouth. "Good dog," Derk said. He smoothed her coat with his hand.

"I must ask you to do something hard, maybe it's the hardest thing you've ever done," Pa said, putting his hand on Derk's shoulder. "We're all fond of Bello, but we can't take her on the ship. No animals are allowed."

Derk bit his lip and nodded. He had prepared himself to take this like a man, but it wasn't working. He stared at the ground, willing himself not to cry.

"I hope you understand, Son."

The next day Derk carried the milk to the cheese maker. Bello ran at his side, racing off now and then to chase a squirrel. His lip was raw from biting it, but biting it kept the tears from flooding his eyes. It wasn't fair, Derk had complained to Ma that morning. "My only friend, Bello, has to stay behind."

"I know, Son," Ma replied. "Life isn't fair. We just have to make the best of it."

She was right, of course. He knew that, but it didn't take away any of the anguish he felt over leaving Bello behind. As he glanced at the dog at his side, tears welled up again.

Derk took the milk to the cheese maker, and then he and Bello walked across the street to Elizabeth's house. She was in the garden, pulling weeds.

Elizabeth stood up as Bello woofed and trotted over to her. "Bello, did you come to see me?" She dropped the weeds and leaned over to scratch between her ears.

Bello looked up at her.

"You're a good dog, Bello."

"Would you..." Derk choked on the words. "Would you like to keep Bello?"

She stared at him, silent.

Derk started again. "I mean, Bello seems to like you."

"She's your dog. I couldn't take her away from you."

Derk shook his head. "I want you to have her."

"You're not making any sense, Derk." She looked down at Bello and ran her hand across the dog's smooth coat.

He had to make Elizabeth understand. Taking a deep breath, he blurted out, "I'm going away!"

She looked up at him, startled. "You're going away? Where? Are you going to…Amerika?"

Derk stared at the ground. "Yes. Bello can't go along."

She leaned down and ran her hand over Bello's fur again and again. It was a long time before she spoke. "I'll keep Bello for you," she said slowly, as if thinking how to form every word. "I'd be glad to keep her…till you come back."

"We're leaving in two weeks. I'll bring her the day before we leave."

She nodded in agreement.

Derk turned and hurried to the street, tasting blood on his lip, trying to control the sobs inside. Bello ran along at his heels. I'll come back, he promised himself. I'm leaving now, but I'll be back.

+ + + + +

"Derk, get up! Have you forgotten we're leaving today?"

He bolted out of bed, dressed, and grabbed a piece of bread

from the table. Outside Pa nailed the covers on the boxes that held dishes, bedding and tools. "And wheat seed for our first crop in Amerika," Pa said, smiling.

Another box held provisions for the trip. They would carry food for the next few days in the market basket. A cloth bag held the family Bible and Ma's Sunday headdress.

"Hurry, Derk. The baggage man is here."

Derk helped load the boxes and baskets, then ran back inside the cottage for one last look. There it was on the mantel, the blue stone that Elizabeth had given him yesterday. He put it into his pocket, along with his jackknife.

"Derk!" Pa stuck his head inside the door.

"Coming!" He ran past Pa and climbed onto the wagon, settling himself among the boxes.

The wagon started with a lurch. Derk stared back at the farmyard, trying to imprint the scene on his mind. It disappeared as they rounded the bend.

A short time later the wagon stopped for Mr. and Mrs. Schutt and their baby. The two families would travel together.

"Derk, rabbit," Martin said, pointing toward the bushes beside the road.

"If Bello were here," Jacobus said, "she'd be chasing that rabbit, wouldn't she, Derk?" Derk shook his head, agreeing, then turned away.

The barge they boarded at Arnhem took them to Rotterdam.

Derk had never seen so many people. They were everywhere, coming and going, boarding ships, loading and unloading cargo.

They sailed on the last day of August. Derk stood on the deck and stared at the shore. So much of what I care about…Bello…Latin school…I'm leaving it all behind.

He wiped his eyes with his sleeve. Will I ever see my dog again? Will I ever get the chance to be a doctor? His dreams turned to mist as he lost sight of the shore.

Part Two
THE JOURNEY

THE ATLANTIC OCEAN, ERIE CANAL,
THE GREAT LAKES

Map from **Wintersvijkse Pioniers in Amerika**, *Willem Wilterdink, 1990*

Chapter 6

Welkom to Amerika! September 1847

Derk clung to the railing of the ship and breathed in the cold, fresh air. Up on deck for the first time since they left Rotterdam, the family felt much better than they had for a week.

A violent storm lashed the ship the first week. Most of the passengers were ill, including Derk's family. Derk decided that the stench from the vomit was far more horrid than all the rotting potatoes back home.

Now he swayed with the pitching and rolling of the ship as it rode across the waves.

"Will we be in West-consin when we get off this big ship?" Jacobus asked.

Pa took off his cap and rubbed his forehead. "No, we'll be in New York. We've a long way to go after we arrive in Amerika."

"Where will we live in West-consin?" Derk asked.

"Remember the families who went to Amerika over a year ago?" Putting his cap on his head, Pa smiled at the boys. "We'll live near them. Their letters say we can make a good life there."

Martin slid out of Ma's arms and ran to Derk. He lifted the toddler, staggering as the ship rolled.

"Pa, what will you like best about West-consin?" Hannah asked.

"Oh, there are many good things," Pa said. "Land is cheap. We can buy a farm twice the size of the one we rented in Winterswyk."

"It will be wonderful to have a place that's our very own," Ma said. "We'll never have to move again."

Pa smiled. "Yes, there's something else – after we own land for five years, we can become citizens. Then we can vote for the president of the country. Think of that. We can choose our lawmakers."

He stroked his beard. "Yes, there's much that's good about West-consin, but the best thing – can you guess what the best thing is?"

"I know, I know," Hannah shouted. "No one will be put in jail for worshiping God!"

Pa nodded his head. "Yes, that will be the best thing."

A cold wind swept the deck. "Brrr," Ma said. "I think it's time to go below and get out of this wind."

The next morning Derk hopped out of his bunk, eager to begin woodcarving lessons. Pa had noticed an elderly man, a Mr. Van Doon, carving as he sat on a bench in the passageway. When Pa asked if he would give Derk help with his new whittling project, he agreed to do so.

Breakfast and then Bible study afterward with Pa seemed to drag on. Derk hadn't memorized the verses, so now he had to say them to Pa. His father had high standards; every word had to be in the right place, not like Ma, who would sometimes accept misplaced words and overlook omissions. After reciting the verses, he ran up on deck to join Mr. Van Doon. Derk found the man sitting behind the small cabin on deck.

"Eh, Derk," Mr. Van Doon greeted him. "I thought you forgot to come, or didn't want to."

"Sorry I'm late," Derk said. "I got delayed." He took out his jackknife and sat down next to him.

The man handed him a chunk of wood. It was a small block of pine, not much bigger than Derk's hand. "What do you want to make?"

"I want to make a rabbit." Derk rubbed the smooth surface. "If it turns out well, I'll give it to my little brother."

Mr. Van Doon pulled a piece of charcoal from a pocket. With it he sketched the outline of a rabbit on the wood. "Start here; shave this wood off first," he said, pointing at the oval back of the rabbit. "Your pa said you're from the Winterswyk area. Are you traveling to West-consin, too?"

"Yes." Derk worked hard, trying to hold the knife steady with the pitching of the ship. Gradually his strokes became more even. He stopped to shake his cramped fingers.

Picking up the rabbit, Mr. Van Doon inspected it. With his knife he smoothed out a spot where Derk's knife had slipped, gouging away too much wood.

"Why are you going to Amerika?" Derk asked. "Do you have a family?"

The man's face crinkled into a smile. "Such questions," he said. Then with a more serious look he added, "Years ago my wife couldn't leave her ailing parents. When they died, she took care of her sister." He made a few strokes with the knife. "My wife died taking care of others. I was the only one left behind. My son and his family live in Amerika."

"In West-consin?"

"Yes, that's where I'm going. Such a big farm my son has, so prosperous he tells me in his letters. Soon I will see for myself, eh, Derk?"

+ + + + +

"Apples! Fresh bread! Apples!" the peddler shouted. "Buy an apple and a loaf of bread!"

The ship had docked in New York City harbor and every peddler had something to sell. Agents from railway and steamship companies were on board, hoping to sign passengers on and get their business. Pa stood in line, waiting to talk with a steamship company agent.

With the other folks from their village, Derk's family was planning to travel north to Albany, and then across New York State to Buffalo on the shores of Lake Erie. There they'd board a steamship and sail the Great Lakes "horseshoe" to Wisconsin.

"Apples! Apples!" the peddler shouted again.

An apple would taste so good, Derk thought. He had no money, but maybe he had something to trade. He searched his pockets.

He found a piece of twine, the stone from Elizabeth, and a gold button from an officer's uniform. In another pocket he found his jackknife. He couldn't trade that away. Mr. Van Doon said that Derk was doing well. Martin loved the rabbit he had made for him, even without the lopsided ear.

Derk walked to the railing, trying to forget how much he wanted an apple. Gazing around the harbor he saw huge ships, rowboats and barges. On the wharf men were loading and unloading cargo. In the distance were warehouses, and beyond, the shops and houses of New York.

Pa, Jacobus, and Mr. Schutt joined Derk at the railing.

"Wagon for hire! Wagon for hire!" a man called. He stepped down from his wagon, tied his horse to a hitching post on the wharf, and started toward the ship. He was wearing a flat cap and breeches. The four watched as the man climbed the gangplank.

"Welkom to America!" The man spoke in Dutch, his smile showing a missing front tooth. He extended a gnarled hand to Pa. "You'll like this country."

Other men gathered around.

The man shook hands with everyone. "Where you from?

"Winterswyk in Gelderland," Pa said.

"Gelderland? Me, too." With his tongue the man shifted the wad of tobacco to his other cheek. "I come here ten years ago. Where you going?"

"West-consin," Pa said.

"West-consin?" the man asked with a puzzled look. "Oh, you mean WIS-consin. It's WIS-consin." He removed his cap, smoothed back his thinning gray hair, and replaced his cap. "How you traveling there?"

"We'll go north to Albany by boat," Pa said.

The man turned and faced the group. "All of you going to Albany?"

The men nodded.

"Got to get your baggage to the steamers on the Hudson. I'll load it on my wagon and deliver it. I'll take good care of you." He looked around the group.

"What do you charge?" Mr. Schutt asked.

"Twenty-five gold coins. You pay fifteen coins when I load it and ten when I unload it." He spit the wad of tobacco onto the deck. Placing the toe of his boot on the wad, he forced it into the cracks in the deck boards.

He continued, "Save you five gold coins if you pay it all when I load your baggage. Cost you only twenty gold coins, then." He took a pouch from his jacket pocket. "You don't want to move those heavy boxes and sea chests by yourself. Won't find any rates cheaper."

"How do we know that our baggage will be at the dock on time?" Mr. Schutt asked.

"Oh, you can trust me," the baggage hauler said. "I'm Dutch, too. I look out for my fellow countrymen." He smiled widely again and then gestured at Mr. Schutt with the pouch. "Can I haul your baggage for you?"

"Yes," Mr. Schutt said.

"And mine," another said.

"Mine, too."

"Good." The man opened the pouch and put a wad of tobacco

into his mouth. "Anyone else?" He paused and looked around. "I'll be here tomorrow morning when the ship's ready to unload." He turned and shuffled down the gangplank.

Derk tugged at his pa's sleeve. "Why didn't you hire him to haul our baggage?"

"I have two boys to help move our boxes," Pa said, as he put an arm around Derk's shoulders. "Besides, you can't trust everyone you meet. They must first prove they can be trusted. Now let's go below and help Ma finish packing and get the boxes closed."

Derk walked slowly down the steps into the hold. How could anyone know who could be trusted in this new land?

Chapter 7

Fire! Fire! November 1847

"Is that our ship, Pa?" Derk asked.

They had come by Erie Canal across New York State to the western end of Lake Erie. Now they were ready to board a Great Lakes vessel that would take them from Buffalo to Wisconsin.

"Can you read the name? Is it the *Phoenix*?"

The flag snapped in the stiff breeze. Derk looked at the name painted on the prow. He spelled it out. "*P-H-O-E-N-I-X.* That's it. Do you suppose this ship is named after the legend of the Phoenix bird? We read about it in school. The bird burns in a fire of its own making and then comes to life again."

"Might be," Pa said. "Thank God the captain waited for us. We'll have enough time to get on board and get settled. It will be good to get to our new home."

Derk looked at Pa carefully. His voice sounded weary — weary from all the miles they had come, weary from all the miles they had to go until they reached Wisconsin. Derk was tired, too. He thought of their friends, the Schutts, who stayed behind in New York City. Their possessions had been stolen by the baggage man. Their baggage was not at the dock, and the warehouse address he had given them was false – an empty field. Had Mr. Schutt found work? Could he save enough money to bring his family to Wisconsin in spring?

The *Phoenix*, glistening in the cold November sunshine, was the last ship that would sail to Wisconsin that season. Ice floes would soon clog the narrow channels that connected the lakes, making it too dangerous for ships to travel safely.

The steamer sailed the next day. Wanting to explore the ship that would be his home for a week or two, Derk talked to Ma.

"Take Martin with you," she suggested. "He needs to move around. A walk would do him good."

The two brothers walked down every passageway. They heard children's voices and turned a corner. Hannah, Jacobus, and a number of other children, were gathered around a man. Derk walked up to Jacobus, who was standing at the back of the circle of children. "Who is that man?" he whispered.

"Shh…he's Mr. Blish. He's teaching us English words."

Mr. Blish smiled at the two newcomers. Derk knew enough English to know the man was asking his name and age.

"I have a son named David," Mr. Blish said. "He's your age, Derk. Why don't you join us?"

+ + + + +

Mr. Blish held classes every day. Pointing to an object, he would say the word and the children would repeat it. Sometimes the children would teach Mr. Blish some Dutch words.

Derk stayed after class one day. "Mr. Blish, does Sheboygan have a school I could attend?"

"I think so. Why do you ask?"

"I attended Latin school, but we left before I got a diploma. In Holland, to go to the university, you have to have a diploma from a Latin school."

"The university?" Mr. Blish asked, his eyes widening. "You're ambitious." Seeing Derk's blank expression, he said, "Am-bi-tious – that just means you have a strong desire, in your case, a strong desire to learn. What do you want to study?"

"Medicine. I want to be a doctor."

"I think you'd make a good doctor. I've seen you care for your little brother. Schools in Sheboygan? I don't know. I'm from Kenosha." He thought a moment, then snapped his fingers. "I can ask the Hazelton sisters; they're returning from a school out East. They would know about schools in their hometown."

So…girls can go to school in Wisconsin, Derk thought. Then he remembered his manners. "Thank you, Mr. Blish."

"You're a good student, Derk. You're doing well with English. And I'll ask the sisters about schools in Sheboygan."

+ + + + +

Derk sat on his bunk with his jackknife, working on the owl he was carving. The beak wasn't turning out right, so he went to find Mr. Van Doon.

The man looked it over and took out his knife. "Sit down." He began working on the beak. "Did you hear that the Captain's been injured?"

"Captain Sweet? How?"

55

"Icy deck. He fell, injured his knee, and can't walk. See how I'm holding the knife? The captain may be staying in his cabin for the rest of the trip."

"Who runs the ship if the captain can't?"

"Oh, there are others who can do it," Mr. Van Doon said. He looked at the owl carefully. "Maybe they can't keep the crew in line like Captain Sweet can, but I think they'll do all right." He took a few more short strokes with the knife.

"What do you mean, keep the crew in line?"

"Don't you worry, Derk. The first mate and the chief engineer can take the captain's place." He handed the owl back to the boy. The beak was perfect.

A few days later the *Phoenix* fought high winds and rough seas as it sailed into Lake Michigan. The steamer took refuge from the furious storm in the harbor in Manitowoc Bay. First, the crew unloaded freight and then brought cordwood on board. Now the ship had enough fuel to reach Chicago, where it would spend the winter. Sheboygan, about twenty-five miles south of Manitowoc, was the next stop. The chief engineer made a decision; the *Phoenix* would not sail until the storm was over.

That evening Pa tucked Derk and Jacobus into the bunk they shared. "Try to get some rest, even in this storm," Pa said. "Tomorrow we'll be in Sheboygan, our new home."

Derk settled down on the bunk, trying to ignore the pitch and roll of the steamer. Violent winds continued to toss the ship back and forth. "Jacobus," he whispered, "Do you feel seasick?"

Jacobus answered with a soft snore.

I hope I can go right to sleep, Derk thought. When he did, he dreamed that Pa and he walked toward a field filled with golden wheat swaying gently in the breeze. Pa's smile showed his satisfaction with the crops on his new farm. Bello trotted along beside them and Derk smiled, too.

+++++

"What...what's the matter?" Was the storm over, or had Derk fallen out of the bunk for the second time that night?

"Get up, Derk," Pa said, shaking him. "Get your shirt and shoes on."

Derk coughed as he sat up. "I smell smoke." He slipped his arms into his shirt.

"There's a fire in the boiler room," Pa said. "It might get out of control."

Derk sat on the edge of the bunk. The acrid smoke penetrated his nostrils. "Fire? How did it start?" he asked.

Pa picked up Derk's shoes and handed them to his son. "After we left Manitowoc, I noticed a strong smell of scorching wood," he said. "Mr. Van Doon, a Mr. O'Connor and I went to the boiler room. Mr. O'Connor told the firemen there was no water in the boiler, but they didn't even look. They just threw more wood into the firebox, and told us to mind our own business."

Derk slipped on his shoes. "How does this Mr. O'Connor know how boilers work?"

"He ran one in a factory in Ireland," Pa said.

Through wisps of smoke, the boy saw others just waking up. His own brothers and sister were getting dressed.

"When Mr. Van Doon said the fire might get out of control, they pushed him down," Pa continued. He picked Martin up.

Ma grabbed Martin's blanket and stuffed it into a bag on her arm.

"Mr. Van Doon? Is he hurt?" Derk asked.

"He'll be all right," Pa said. "Put your cap on and follow me."

The family clambered up the stairs after Pa. Clouds of smoke rolled across the deck. Leading them through the smoke, Pa took them to the far corner. Others already waited nearby, their eyes filled with fear. Some women who were cabin passengers rushed past them, screaming in terror as they tried to find the place farthest from the fire.

Between billows of smoke, Derk glimpsed little flames of fire licking through the floor boards. The boiler room was just below the flames.

"Wait here," Pa said, handing Martin to Ma. "I'll help with the bucket brigade."

The heat from the searing wood came into Derk's lungs with every breath. He coughed so hard he thought he would choke.

An alarm pierced the air. Martin started crying and reached for Derk. Ma put her arms around Hannah and Jacobus.

In a few minutes Pa returned, followed by Mr. Blish.

"Too late." Mr. Blish shook his head. "Too late."

A deckhand ran past. Mr. Blish grabbed his arm. "Lifeboats. Launch the lifeboats!"

"Get your hands off me!" The deckhand swore as he pulled himself free of Mr. Blish's grasp. "You're not the captain!" He muttered something under his breath, then ran off.

Mr. Blish looked around and pointed. "Lifeboat! Come on!" He dashed toward it and Derk's family followed.

"Clear the way! Clear the way!"

Derk saw two men carrying a man up the stairs and out on the deck. It was Captain Sweet.

The lifeboat swung into place and those nearest swarmed into it.

"Save room for the Captain!" the First Mate shouted. The men set the injured captain into the boat.

"This one's full!" Mr. Blish yelled. Sailors swung it over the side of the ship and lowered it into the water.

The crew readied the second lifeboat. Again those nearest swarmed into it, fighting for a spot to sit. Someone bumped an older man and he fell to the deck. Pa helped him up.

"No! No! No!"

Derk heard Mr. Blish's voice and looked toward the other end of the boat. A father was trying to get his family, all seven of them, into the already crowded boat.

Mr. Blish took charge. "Don't overload it! It'll sink! There's room for two youngsters."

He looked around, then pointed at Derk, who was holding Martin's hand. "Derk, you and your little brother, get into the boat."

Chapter 8

"Row with The Oars You Got"
November 21, 1847

Derk looked at his parents and back to Mr. Blish. "What about them?" he asked.

"They'll be on the next boat!" Mr. Blish roared. Grabbing Derk under the arms, Mr. Blish lifted him into the lifeboat.

Ma set Martin on Derk's lap and handed him a heavy canvas bag. "God go with you, Sons."

"There's another boat!" Mr. Blish was shouting again, this time at a young woman climbing into the boat. He turned to the sailors who held the ropes. "Move this boat out!"

"Take care of Martin!" Pa cried out over the roar of the fire. "Wait for us on shore!"

The boat swung over the edge of the ship and wobbled on the ropes as it was lowered, hitting the surface with a great splash. Freezing water flew everywhere. Martin screamed and lunged forward, trying to escape the icy spray, but Derk tightened his grip on Martin and hung on.

Burning cinders rained all around them, on jackets, trousers and hair. A husky man behind them snatched a hot coal from Martin's blanket and threw it into the lake. The sailors unfastened the tackle and the deckhands raised it back up to the ship. "Let's go," one sailor shouted, looking around. "The oars! Where are the oars?" He brushed a burning ember from his jacket. "Who's got the oars?"

"Here's one." The husky man handed him an oar from the back of the boat.

"Where's the other one?" The sailor looked up toward the ship. "HELP! HELP!"

"They'll never hear you," the other sailor yelled. "Here's a broom!"

Using the oar and the broom the sailors rowed away from the burning steamer. At last they were out of reach of the falling sparks.

Martin screamed for Ma. Derk tried to quiet him, but it was impossible.

Looking back at the steamer, he saw Ma and Jacobus at the railing. "Look, Martin," Derk said, "there's Ma and Jacobus. See them?"

They stood at the railing, silhouetted against the orange and scarlet flames.

Martin stopped crying when he saw them, but suddenly they left the railing without waving good-bye.

"Mama! Mama!"

"Martin, they're getting into the lifeboat now," Derk said. "We'll see them on shore." He wrapped the blanket around Martin and pulled the screaming child to his chest.

Someone behind them gasped, a long, drawn out sound and Derk looked around. Pointing at the bottom of the boat, a man shouted, "The boat's leaking! We're taking on water! It's leaking!"

Derk looked down and moved his foot. Water splashed into his shoe.

"God in heaven, be merciful," an older woman sobbed. "God, be merciful."

The man took off his shoe and scooped water from the bottom of the boat. He dumped it over the side and scooped again. Others followed his lead. Scoop. Dump. Scoop. Dump.

The water continued to rise. Balancing Martin on just one of his legs, Derk reached down and took off his shoe. Bending over, he scooped up some water.

"Ahh," Martin squealed, wobbling back and forth on Derk's leg.

Derk straightened up to steady his brother and bumped the man's arm as he came up with a shoe full of water. It splashed over their trousers and jackets.

"Just take care of that child," the man said, scowling.

Derk put his shoe on and wrapped both arms around the shrieking child. Feeling the cold and wet from Martin's jacket against his chest reminded Derk of what Pa had said. Derk's most important duty was to take care of Martin.

The man beside Derk put his face up close to Martin's face and said, "Stop your screaming!"

The toddler stopped, but he couldn't stop the gasps that racked his small body.

Looking back at the ship, Derk drew in his breath sharply as the flames reached higher and higher into the sky. Men tossed furniture and parts of cabins into the lake to use as makeshift rafts.

Two young women stood at the ship's railing. Derk guessed that they might be the sisters whose parents owned a hotel in Sheboygan. Why aren't they getting into a lifeboat, Derk wondered.

"Look at the man on the railing," someone shouted. "He's going to jump!"

"Thank God he made it," someone said, as the man landed on the floating door.

The two girls climbed onto the railing, clasped hands, and jumped together. Missing the raft, they sank beneath the surface and didn't come up again.

Derk closed his eyes. He didn't want to see anyone else jump. "God, take care of my family," he whispered.

Martin looked at Derk's closed eyes. "Derk, open up," he said, trying to pry open his brother's eyes with his small fingers. Derk opened his eyes and wrapped his arms more tightly around his brother.

"The fire must be getting worse," a man beside Derk said; "they're climbing the rigging. That's not safe."

Flames followed at their heels. Derk knew what was next; they'd soon fall into the fire below. He wiped his eyes with his sleeve.

"The fire must have spread over the whole deck," the man beside Derk said. "I wonder where the next lifeboat is. It should be following us to shore."

Derk wondered, too. Did my family get into the boat? Did something bad happen to them? He shook his head, trying to keep those thoughts away.

A cold wind blew across the boat and Martin shivered. Unbuttoning his own jacket, Derk drew his brother close to his chest. Then he wrapped the jacket over him and buttoned Martin inside. A woman put a blanket over them as the child snuggled against his brother.

The men continued bailing, but the frigid waters kept rising, now swirling higher, now gripping Derk's ankles like icy fingers.

BOOM! BOOM! Louder than the loudest thunder, the explosion echoed across the water. BOOM! BOOM! Derk turned and looked at the ship. Flames streamed far out upon the water. The raging fire lit up the sky like daylight.

"All is lost," a man said, shaking his head. "All is lost."

Derk wondered if any of those makeshift rafts or the lifeboats had been touched by the flames that shot out from the steamer. As they neared the shore, their boat ran aground in shallow water.

"Everyone out!" The sailor got out and steadied the boat as the passengers stood up. Derk tried to stand, then remembered that Martin was still buttoned inside his jacket. As he fumbled with the buttons, the sailor yelled at him to hurry.

The husky man took Martin from Derk's arms and carried him to the beach. Derk clambered over the side of the boat and waded to shore. The icy water sent needles through his legs. He shuddered, thinking of the two young women who jumped into the waves together.

65

The sailors shoved off and started back toward the ship. Would they get there? Who would bail water?

A fire was burning on the beach. Captain Sweet, with his out-stretched leg sat on a stump near the fire. Men gathered sticks, branches and old boards and threw them on the flames.

Derk fell on the frozen sand close to the fire and Martin slumped beside him. Where was his family? "God, I'll never be mean to Jacobus again," Derk whispered. "I'll never tease him or play tricks on him again."

He turned as he heard shouts behind him. Villagers, seeing fire and smoke on the lake, came to the shore. Some brought hot food; some carried blankets.

"What's the name of this town and how far are we from She-boygan?" Captain Sweet asked. He rubbed his knee with his hand.

"About ten miles north," one man replied. "This is Seven Mile Creek and the village is Haven."

"I need a horse and buggy to take me to a doctor," the captain said. "I can't walk, can't bend my leg."

"I have a horse and buggy," the man said. He threw another board on the fire. "I can take you to Sheboygan. We don't have a doctor in our town, but one there should be able to help you."

Martin finished his bread and cheese. He climbed onto Derk's lap, snuggled against him and fell asleep. His brother laid him on a blanket near the fire, then covered him with another blanket.

Derk looked out at the lake and watched the returning lifeboats.

Would they get there in time to rescue the others? He glanced toward the south. A large ship steamed toward the *Phoenix*.

"Thank God," the husky man said. "That ship will rescue everyone." He introduced himself as Mr. Willink.

Along with those on shore, Derk watched as the boat sailed close to the *Phoenix*. They waited for what seemed like hours before the ship sailed south, towing the smoking hull of the steamer.

"Are you ready to walk to Sheboygan, Derk?" Mr. Willink asked. Your brother's lucky; I'll carry him. Too bad Captain Sweet didn't hire a wagon. There was no room for anyone else in that buggy."

Derk looked out across the lake. "My pa told me to meet him on the beach."

"The big boat rescued them. Your family will be in Sheboygan, waiting for you."

Mr. Willink picked Martin up and they set off, following the others. The trail lay close to the lake and wound through stands of evergreen forest. They passed small clearings and cabins. Pungent smoke rose from the chimneys.

Derk felt a sharp, stabbing pain in his side. The pain had been there since they left Haven. Now it was much worse. He fell farther and farther behind, until doubling over in pain, he stopped.

Mr. Willink turned around and walked back to Derk. "Are you all right? Do you need to rest? Maybe sitting down will make the pain go away.

Derk sat down next to the trail. Mr. Willink put Martin down and rubbed his shoulders. After a few minutes they heard the neigh of horses and the rumble of a wagon.

The horses and wagon, coming from the south, stopped next to them. "Would you like a ride to town?" the man asked. "Climb into the wagon by the others."

Derk climbed on the wagon. Two women, one older, one younger with a baby, sat on the straw.

Mr. Willink lifted Martin onto the wagon. "Lay down on the straw, Martin," he said. "You lay down, too, Derk. You need some rest."

He curled up next to his brother on the straw and Mr. Willink covered them with the blanket. Derk woke when the wagon jolted to a stop at the harbor in Sheboygan. When he sat up he could see the smoking ruins of the *Phoenix*. The hull had burned to the water's edge. Nearby was the big boat that towed the steamer to the harbor.

The beach was crowded. It seemed like everyone in Sheboygan had come to the waterfront. Some people were handing out blankets and others had food.

"Will you stay with Martin while I look for my family?" Derk asked Mr. Willink. "I don't want to wake him. He's so tired."

He nodded. "Martin and I will wait for you right here, on the wagon."

Derk pushed his way though the crowd, looking for his pa. It seemed like it would be impossible to find him in this sea of flat caps and wide breeches.

Back and forth through the throng he went, looking at those sitting on blankets and checking circles of people for a glimpse of his family.

He came to the water's edge. No family. No one. Then he spied Mr. Van Doon sitting on the beach, alone. Derk sped across the sand to him, eyes brimming with tears. "I'm so glad to see you!" he cried, throwing himself down in front of his friend.

"Derk!" The man coughed, turned his head and spit.

"Did you see my family? Where is the lifeboat they were on? Did the big boat pick them up? Where are they?" The questions tumbled from Derk's lips.

"Not so fast, Derk, my boy, not so fast," Mr. Van Doon said, hacking away. "Sit down beside me."

Derk sat beside him.

The man gasped for air. "Yes, I saw your parents." He took a deep breath. "Your family got into the lifeboat."

"Good! Good!" Derk stood up, craned his neck and scanned the crowd again. "Where are they now?"

"Not so fast," Mr. Van Doon said. His cough sounded like a dog's bark. "I swallowed some lake water when I jumped overboard."

Derk crouched in front of his friend on the sand and looked at him. His face was pale. He seemed weak. The boy waited for him to speak.

"I can't seem to get the water out," the man said, pounding his chest and whooping.

Derk patted his shoulder.

"The lifeboat...." Mr. Van Doon started and faltered.

"Yes, yes?"

"Your family got into the lifeboat with other folks. It was lowered into the lake. A young man rushed up to the railing." Mr. Van Doon stopped and coughed. He cleared his throat and spit. "The fire must have made the man crazy with fear. He jumped from the railing and landed in the boat." He coughed again.

Derk peered into Mr. Van Doon's eyes as he squatted in front of him. "Go on, go on!"

"He hit it with such force...that it turned over." He drew in his breath sharply. "I'm sorry, Derk... there was nothing I could do." He covered his face with his hands. "All those in the boat...went down."

Derk fell to the ground in a crumpled heap.

Part Three

SHEBOYGAN COUNTY, WISCONSIN

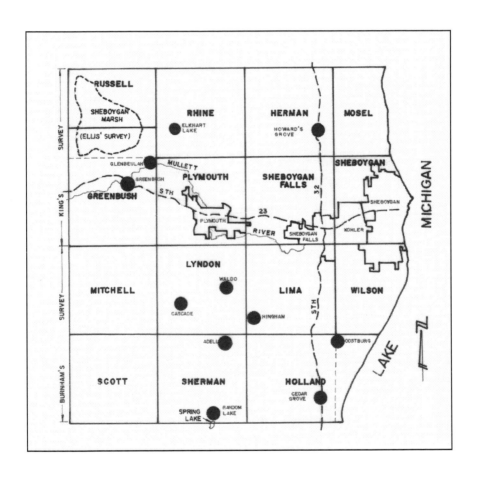

Chapter 9

Dear Ones... January 1848 – May 1848

January 28, 1848

Dear Uncle Willem and Uncle Johannes,

I wish I had not come to America. Only bad things have happened since I came. I am all alone and deserted here. Pa and Ma, Jacobus and Hannah were drowned when the steamer we traveled on caught fire and burned. They got into a lifeboat, but it tipped over and all of them went down. Martin and I got to shore in another boat.

We are living with the Van Doon family. I met Mr. Van Doon on board ship as we crossed the ocean. His son, Elwood, lives near Sheboygan. He moved here two years ago from Holland. There are seven children in the family. Martin gets along well with Mrs. Van Doon and the other children. They all like him.

I am asking you, as my only relatives, to send money so Martin and I can return to Holland. I get only my food and a bed here. I help with all the farm chores, feeding livestock and splitting wood.

I want to come back and attend the university, and become a doctor, like you, Uncle Willem. Please send money so we can come back home.

Derk

May 30, 1848

Elizabeth,

It is very difficult to write this letter. Maybe you heard that the steamer we were on caught fire....

...A man that I met on the ship on the ocean, Mr. Van Doon, was rescued, too. He took us to live with him on his son's farm near Sheboygan. The Van Doons have been good to Martin and me. The wife wants to keep Martin as her own son; I think he reminds her of her baby boy who died three years ago. With seven children plus Martin, they don't have room for me.

Mr. Van Doon, the grandpa, got sick after he was rescued from the icy water; he never recovered and died last month.

I am leaving the Van Doons tomorrow. Elwood Van Doon arranged for me to work for a man named Smith. He runs a fishing business on the shore of Lake Michigan. I hope to save enough money to come back to our village. Then I will go to the university to become a doctor.

I try not to think about Winterswyk or Bello, so far away. I will come back to visit Martin at the Van Doons and hope to find a letter from you.

Derk

Chapter 10

Gone Fishing   May 31, 1848

"Whoa!" Elwood Van Doon called to the horse as he and Derk pulled up to a fishing shanty on Lake Michigan. A dog came out, yapping, and a man with a knife in his hand poked his head out of the shanty door.

"I've brought you a worker," Van Doon shouted, climbing down from the wagon.

Derk sat staring at the choppy waves on the lake, not more than forty feet away. He hadn't been this close to the lake, hadn't even seen the lake, since…the fire. His hands turned clammy and cold sweat poured down his body.

"Get down, Derk."

He heard and understood the voice, but could not act. He seemed to be in the middle of a nightmare, knowing that if he didn't run, the enemy would strike and he would perish. He was unable to move; he could not have run, even if he had wanted to do so.

"Derk, get out of the wagon." The voice broke through the nightmare.

The boy shook his head to clear away the awful picture. Standing up slowly, he walked to the side of the wagon and climbed over.

The man disappeared into the shanty and then reappeared without the knife. Walking toward the wagon, he wiped his bloody hands on his pants, then put out his hand to Derk. The boy shook his hand, hoping he wasn't touching any blood.

"Name is Gilbert T. Smith. To you, I'm Mr. Smith. Your name?" Silence.

"His name is Derk," Mr. Van Doon offered.

"He's mighty small and skinny for thirteen, puny…yes, that's the word, puny." Mr. Smith looked at Elwood Van Doon over Derk's head. "Didn't you feed him? A nor'easter will blow him away."

Derk shifted his weight from one foot to the other and stared at his feet.

"He's a good worker," Van Doon said. "He's helped with cutting down trees, clearing land, and planting crops at our farm."

"Well, we'll give Derk a try. We'll see what he can do. I'm right in the middle of cleaning the day's catch. Put your bag in the cabin over there, Derk." He jerked his head toward a cabin partly hidden by the trees. "I'll show you how to dress fish." He started back to the shanty.

Mr. Van Doon climbed into the wagon and picked up the reins. "Godspeed, Derk," he called. The boy watched the wagon as it climbed the hill and disappeared from sight.

"Derk!" Mr. Smith stuck his head out of the shanty. "Hurry! We've no time for loafing today."

Derk dashed toward the cabin, then stopped abruptly. The mangy dog darted out of the trees, barking furiously.

"I know," he said to the dog. "You're just protecting your master. Come on, nice dog, nice dog." Reaching into his pocket he found the crust of bread Mrs. Van Doon had given him for lunch. He ripped it in half and held it out to the dog.

The mongrel snatched the crust and wolfed it down, then looked up, asking for more. Derk got out the remaining bread, gave it to the dog, then bent over to pet him. "Nice dog, nice dog," he said in a soothing voice. The dog licked his hand.

Mr. Smith came around the side of the shanty. "Don't waste time with the dog," he said to Derk. "Fido, go lay down."

Derk ran to the cabin, pushed open the door, and set his bag against the wall. He raced to the shanty, followed by Fido, who lay down in the sun at the door.

"Ever done anything like this before?" Mr. Smith asked.

Derk shook his head. "Not often. My ma usually cleaned the fish I caught."

Mr. Smith took a fish from a wooden box. "Watch, I'll show you how to do this. See this whitefish…it's about four pounds or so…." He laid the fish on its side on a wooden table. "This is as big as they get…a prize fish…most are smaller." With a stroke of the knife, he sliced open its belly from head to tail. With his left hand he pried the flesh open.

"See, now I place the knife up here by the head and against the backbone and scrape all the way to the tail." He held up the fish and dumped the entrails into a heap on the table. Tossing the fish into a barrel, he turned to Derk. "Here's a knife." He picked up another knife and grabbed a fish from the box.

"Stand over there." He pointed to the opposite side of the table.

Derk took a small fish from the container and laid it on its side. Anchoring the fish with his left hand, he put the knife at the head and slowly drew it down toward the tail. His hand wobbled and he stopped at the mid-point of the fish.

"You can't quit now!" Then in a more encouraging voice, the man said, "Keep trying. You'll soon get the hang of it."

Derk repositioned the knife. This time he drew the knife to the tail. Opening the flesh, he scraped out the insides.

"You missed some guts. It's got to be clean."

The boy put the knife back at the head and drew it to the tail, this time catching most of what he missed the first time. With a few more strokes of the knife, the flesh was clean. He looked away and coughed. After placing the fish in the barrel, Derk looked in the box for another small fish. He picked up and rejected four large fish, then found a smaller one. Halfway through the afternoon when the fish were cleaned, salted and packed in barrels, they stopped to eat. Derk followed Mr. Smith to the cabin.

He stood at the door and looked around. In the center of the dirt floor stood a crude table surrounded by blocks of wood serving as chairs. A built-in bed stood in one corner, and a stone fireplace took up the opposite wall. A ladder led to a loft and a gun hung over the mantel on the fireplace.

Mr. Smith reached up on the mantel. He took some smoked fish and placed them on the table. Picking up a loaf of bread, he held it against his chest and sliced it, laying each slice on a dirty plate on the table.

He picked up a fish, broke off the head and tail and put it between two slices of bread. "Here you are, Fido," he said as he threw the head and tail outside the cabin door. Pouring some dark brown liquid from a jug into two cups, he pushed one toward Derk.

Following his lead, Derk made a sandwich for himself. He gave the head and tail of the fish to Fido, who was waiting with his tongue hanging out.

"You'll have to help me with these fish guts," Mr. Smith said as they walked back to the shanty.

Together they tugged and pulled the heavy barrel, dragging it across the sand to the water's edge. Mr. Smith turned the barrel over and dumped the entrails into the lake.

"Do you always do this with the guts?" Derk hoped he wouldn't lose his meal in front of Mr. Smith.

"Sometimes I bury 'em, but there's not enough time today. You can dig some holes tomorrow while I go to Sheboygan to sell the fish."

Derk heard sea gulls. Looking up, he saw them circling lower and lower, trying to get at the free lunch.

Mr. Smith strode ahead to the smokehouse. As Derk stepped inside, he saw racks and racks of fish overhead. They took them down and packed them into boxes.

The next morning after loading boxes of smoked fish and barrels of salted fish onto the wagon, Mr. Smith hitched up the horse. He picked up the reins. "Get those holes dug, Derk, three or four of 'em, where I showed you. Make 'em deep, as deep as the shovel is high. I'll be back in a day or two."

He clucked his tongue to the horse and the wagon rolled off.

Chapter 11

The Grudge   June 1848

Derk woke with a start. For the first moment he didn't know where he was. The air was hot and close. He sniffed. Was that smoke he smelled? He sniffed the air again. Smoke? No. Fire? No.

It was the nightmare – the fire eating away the boards of the deck, the fire getting closer and closer – no lifeboat. He had to make a choice – die in the fire or jump overboard. That's when he'd wake up. Now he fell back on the straw mattress, relieved to find he was in no danger.

The gentle lapping of the waves against the pier and the bobbing of the boats on the water calmed Derk's pounding heart. The gentle sounds had lulled him to sleep these past few nights. The lake, no longer rough and choppy, seemed much less threatening now.

Derk felt so comfortable that he had taken the rowboat out a few times, first staying close to shore. Two days ago he had put out from shore, dropped a line and caught some fish for supper. He hadn't been fishing…since that day with Pieter….

Pieter! So long ago, so far away, but Derk felt anger rising in him when he thought of Pieter. How could he break his promise of being my best friend? Derk asked himself. When I needed a friend the most -- when my pa was in jail -- at that time he betrayed me! The scoundrel!

Something stirred at Derk's feet and brought him back to the present. Fido. Derk smiled, thinking about how he had coaxed the dog up the ladder to the loft.

After Mr. Smith had left, Derk and Fido went to the beach to play fetch. Fido, barking and wagging his tail, brought the stick back each time. When Fido ran to fetch the stick, Derk closed his eyes and pictured himself back home, playing with Bello.

Between playing with Fido, Derk dug two holes to bury the entrails. He finished two more the next day, wanting them to be ready when Mr. Smith returned. Now, three days later, Mr. Smith had not come back. Derk hoped that nothing bad had happened.

His thoughts raced…what would happen to him if Mr. Smith did not come back? The Van Doons were the only folks he knew in Wisconsin, and they didn't have room for him.

His two uncles in the Netherlands? A recent letter from Uncle Willem didn't offer any hope. Derk drew the crumpled envelope from his pocket and read it again.

March 1, 1848

Derk,

…Misfortune has happencd here, too. Uncle Johannes suddenly fell ill about a month ago and has not recovered as expected. Stay in West-consin. There must be a university there where you can study medicine.

He put the letter back into his pocket. Uncle Willem had said nothing about money for a return trip. "If I had the money, I'd go back right now," he told Fido as he stroked the dog's back.

His stomach growled. He and Fido had finished the stale bread and fish yesterday. Maybe he could find a few stray fish in the smoke-house. If not, he'd catch some at the dock for breakfast, then take the boat out, and fish all day.

He climbed down the ladder and tried to coax Fido from the loft. "Come on, Fido, come on." Derk heard a horse's neigh, followed by footsteps outside. Fido barked and jumped to the floor.

Derk glanced at the door. Who might be out there?

Someone knocked. "Anyone home?" a man's voice called. Another knock.

Derk opened the door a crack. A man and a boy stood outside. Derk judged the boy to be about his own age, maybe a year older.

"Hello! I hope we didn't scare you." The man smiled. "Do you understand English?"

Derk nodded.

"Good. I'm Mr. Daane and this is my son, Peter. Mr. Smith sent us. May we come in?"

Can I trust them, Derk wondered, remembering Pa's words about not trusting someone until they had proven themselves trustworthy. They must know Mr. Smith, since he sent them. They seemed friendly. He opened the door. "Come in."

Fido growled and Derk smoothed his coat. "It's all right, Fido." He motioned for them to sit down.

"Mr. Smith asked us to come. He won't be back for some weeks. We want you to come and live with us."

"You want me to stay with you? I don't think I can do that. I'm working for Mr. Smith."

"Mr. Smith broke his leg," Mr. Daane said. "He won't be coming back for some time. He asked us to take you to live with us."

"But Mr. Van Doon brought me here to work. He expects me to be here." Fido's tail brushed his leg. "And what about the dog?"

"We'll tell the Van Doon family; sometimes they attend the same worship services we do. We can take the dog along."

"I have to think about this," Derk said. "How far from here do you live? Could I come back to work for Mr. Smith when he gets well? I'm trying to save money so I can go back home."

Mr. Daane cleared his throat. "We live just three to four miles up the road. I can't pay you, but if you work for me, I'll give you room and board. You can work with Peter clearing land this summer."

He had no other choice. Derk climbed the ladder to the loft and got his jacket. He checked his pockets – gold button, twine, stone, jackknife, letter from his uncle. Everything was there. He took a last look around the cabin and picked up his bag. "Come on, Fido." He closed the cabin door.

Derk looked around the property. The Daanes helped him put the small boat inside the fish shanty, then made certain that the larger one was well anchored at the shore. Derk closed the fish shanty door and braced it shut with a heavy piece of firewood.

The two boys climbed onto the buckboard and sat down on the straw. Peter picked up a long oat straw, pulled down the outer covering and found the clean end. He stuck it in his mouth, then picked up a second straw. "Want one, Derk?" He pulled the outer covering off, then handed it to him.

Derk put it in his mouth and chewed on it. It wasn't breakfast, but it softened his hunger pangs.

Mr. Daane clucked his tongue at the horses and the wagon started. Fido ran along at the side.

"You came here half a year ago, right?" Peter asked. "You know a lot of English words for being here just a short time."

"A man on the steamer taught English to us every day. Do you go to school?"

"I wish I could. I went to school when my family lived in New York State, before we moved here. There's a school in Cedar Grove, a few miles from here, but it's too far away to walk every day. I have books at home that I use."

"Do you have a Latin book?"

"Why do you want to learn Latin?" Peter asked.

"I want to be a doctor."

"Oh, that's a good reason," Peter said. "We need doctors in this state. I think we'll see a lot more folks moving here since Wisconsin became a state last month."

$$+ + + + +$$

Derk found it easy to settle into a routine at the Daane home-stead. Each morning he helped milk the cows before they were put out to eat grass. Often they wandered deep into the forest as they grazed among the trees.

During the day Derk and Peter helped cut down trees and saw them into logs with a crosscut saw. The smaller branches were sawed into shorter lengths and stacked for fuel for the fireplace. They chopped out the smaller stumps and Mr. Daane burned the larger ones.

"It's time to go looking for the cows," Peter said to Derk one late afternoon. He got the gun from the cabin. "Maybe I can shoot some game for tomorrow's dinner. I hope Molly is grazing so we can hear her bell."

Derk whistled for Fido and the dog bounded up to him, ready to go. Peter led them down a winding path, deep into the forest. He stopped. "Shh, I think I hear a bell." He pointed. "The cows are in that direction."

The boys walked on and Fido chased a squirrel up a tree. Peter raised the gun and brought it down with one shot. He handed the gun to Derk, then picked up the squirrel and carried it. They followed the path as they picked their way among the roots of a huge tree. On the other side they stopped abruptly. Ahead, and not far away, stood a large gray animal with its back toward them. Its head was down toward the ground.

"It's a wolf!" Peter whispered. Fido growled.

"Quick! Up a tree!" Peter hissed, running toward the nearest tree. He threw the squirrel over a limb, then grabbing the lowest branch, swung himself up into the tree.

Derk turned around, tripped over a tree root and fell face down. He screamed and Fido barked as the wolf turned and looked at them.

"Come on, Derk!" Peter jumped down from the tree and helped Derk up. Derk grabbed Fido. Together they scrambled up the tree, climbing into the lower branches. The wolf stood there, looking at them.

"Whew! We're safe!" Peter said, catching his breath. "Where's the gun?"

"Oh, no!"

"I thought you had it."

"It's lying down there." Derk pointed. "I must have dropped it when I tripped."

"That's all right; we're safe," Peter said. He paused. "Strange, I expected the wolf to attack us. We'd be an easy supper for it."

The wolf turned and put its head down and went back to whatever was lying on the ground. The boys sat in silence for a few minutes as they watched the animal.

"We could be here all night if that wolf decides to hang around here," Peter said. "I could sneak down and get the gun."

The wolf lifted its head again, then ran off, crashing through the small trees and bushes.

"We didn't need the gun," Derk said, laughing. "Just the mere mention of a gun in the hands of 'Peter the Great Hunter' made the wolf run away.'

Peter laughed. "No, your screaming scared it away," he said. "You screeched so loud I thought the wolf was chewing on your leg. From now on, when I need protection from a wild animal, I'll just ask you to scream."

Derk chuckled. "I guess I was loud. Do you think it'll come back?"

"It's strange that it just stood there. I bet it was eating something. Let's go look; it should be safe now."

They slid down the tree, got Fido down and picked up the gun. Peter led, walking cautiously toward the spot. As they got closer, they could see a carcass. It was a half-eaten hog.

"We'll have a story to tell at supper tonight," Peter said. "Good thing it didn't attack one of our cows."

"I think I hear Molly's bell," Derk said.

"I hear it, too."

They found the cows and then followed them as the animals headed toward the barn.

"Hey, Derk, who is this Elizabeth you know?" Peter asked.

Startled, Derk stumbled over a tree root, then regained his balance. How did Peter know about her? Had he said something about Elizabeth taking care of Bello, and he didn't remember it?

Peter went on. "And who is this Pieter? I thought at first you were talking about me, but then I figured out it was someone else."

"I never said anything about a Pieter."

"Yes, you did."

"I did not! You're making this up!"

"No, I'm not. Do you want to know the truth?"

Derk stared at him.

"You talk in your sleep, Derk."

"Woof!" Fido ran toward a cow that was straggling behind and brought her back to the herd.

"I...I talk in my sleep?"

"Almost every night. Seems to me you're holding a grudge against this Pieter. What happened between you two?"

"It's nothing."

"If you don't tell me, that's all right," Peter said, "but my pa always says, 'when you hold a grudge, you put two people in prison cells.' "

+ + + + +

The rest of the summer flew by, filled with clearing land, picking blackberries in the woods for Mrs. Daane's pies, and playing with Fido. Nearly every evening Peter tutored Derk in English. By the end of the summer he could read and write English well.

One Sunday in late summer, Mr. Daane hitched his horse to the buckboard and took Derk to visit Martin at the Van Doons. As they rode back to the Daane's home, Derk reflected on his visit. He was almost sorry he had gone to visit Martin. They'd been separated for just four months, and Martin didn't seem to remember they were brothers. The youngster hung unto Mrs. Van Doon until Derk asked him if he had a toy rabbit. Martin smiled and showed the rabbit to him.

Derk asked Mrs. Van Doon how Martin was getting along.

"He's just like my own son," she said. "He and Kees...they're always together."

That's good, Derk thought. At least, Martin has a home. Maybe Martin could stay in Wisconsin with the Van Doon's when he went back to Winterswyk. He had another disappointment – no letter from Elizabeth.

It would soon be fall, and though he'd had a good summer with the Daanes, he was getting restless. The land was cleared and he knew the family didn't have work for him in the months ahead. Although Mr. Smith was back at his fishing business, he didn't have anything for Derk to do in winter.

A preacher who stopped to visit the Daanes told Derk about the new village of Greenbush and the Wade House Inn. A stagecoach ran between two larger towns, Sheboygan and Fond du Lac, with the noon stop at the halfway point, the Wade House in Greenbush.

Mr. Sylvanus Wade was a "forward-looking " man with new ideas, like starting a school with advanced classes. Maybe Derk could get a diploma there. A new sawmill, built by a Wade son-in-law, was in operation in the hamlet. Maybe Derk could learn a trade, like black-smithing, from Mr. Wade.

Mr. Daane needed some supplies from Sheboygan and Derk could ride with him. From there he would catch the stagecoach to Greenbush.

"Thank you for giving me a place to live this summer," Derk told the family after breakfast. "You made me feel welcome the first day. And a special thanks to you, Peter, for teaching me English."

Peter turned to Derk and put his hands on Derk's shoulders. "Promise you'll come back and visit," he said. "I promise."

Chapter 12

Off to Greenbush   Fall 1848

Derk held onto the railing of the driver's seat on the stage-coach, half afraid that he would fall off the high perch. The driver, Mr. John Frink, held the reins as they bounced along through the ruts, over tree roots and around stumps. The stage had left Sheboygan early that morning and Derk's bones ached and his insides seemed to slosh with every bounce.

"Someday there'll be a plank road all the way from Sheboygan to Greenbush," the driver said. "Now that Wisconsin's a state, I've had more passengers. It's been good for business."

He reached down and picked up a long tin pipe from behind his feet. "Here, Derk, take this horn and blow it." He handed him a straight hollow metal pipe, slightly flared at one end. It was about four feet long and awkward to hold. "We're just one half hour away from the Wade

House Inn. We have to let them know that it's time to get our dinner ready. Just blow it, Derk."

The boy placed the horn to his lips, took a deep breath and blew. A weak sound came out. "How can the folks at the Wade House hear this horn? It doesn't seem loud enough."

"They don't hear it," the driver said.

"Then why should I blow it?"

"The dogs hear it, and they let everyone know that we're coming."

"Ohh, they bark."

"Howl is more like it. When the horn sounds, it hurts their ears and they howl. Hasn't failed yet. Biscuits are always coming out of the oven when we get there."

Derk blew the horn once more; maybe the dogs hadn't heard it. He didn't want to be responsible for the dinner not being ready for the seven passengers in the coach. He laid the horn on the platform at his feet.

The howling dogs made Derk think about Fido. He missed the dog, but he couldn't take him along. A dog might not be welcome at the Inn. Derk might not be welcome either. Would Mr. Wade need another farm hand to bring in the fall harvest, or split wood, or care for the horses?

"Slow, Boys, steady, steady," Mr. Frink said. The four horses slowed to a walk as the stage rocked down a steep hill and around a large tree stump.

A short time later the stagecoach rounded the bend and Derk saw a clearing in the woods. A log house with an addition on the back stood at the front of the clearing.

The driver pointed. "That's the inn. Over there's the blacksmith shop. Just beyond is the new sawmill. Should be plenty of work for you to do here." He smiled at Derk. "And when you want to go back to Sheboygan, just hop on board when I'm coming through. Look, that's Sylvanus Wade now, just coming out of the inn."

Derk saw a man with a ruff of a beard running under his chin and going from ear to ear. Wearing black pants and a vest over a long-sleeved white shirt, he didn't look the part of a frontiersman.

"Sylvanus Wade lived in New England before coming to Wisconsin," Mr. Frink said. "He's a Yankee, not the usual settler you find out here." He paused. "I'll need a fresh team before going to Fond du Lac. Stay close; I'll introduce you to Mr. Wade."

The driver slowed the horses and then stopped in front of the inn. A young man placed a wooden stool on the ground in front of the coach door. He opened the door and Mr. Wade began helping the passengers out and escorting them inside.

Mr. Frink drove the empty stage around to the back of the inn where another young man unhitched the stage and tied up the horses.

"Andrew, this is Derk Van Vliet," the driver said. "Andrew is the oldest son of Sylvanus Wade. Derk's hoping to find work with your father."

"What can you do?" Andrew Wade asked.

Derk clutched his knapsack to his chest, forgetting all he had

93

planned to say. "I helped on a farm this summer," he mumbled.

"Doing what?"

"Ah…"

"Tell him what you told me, Derk," Mr. Frink said. "You helped clear land, split wood and care for the livestock."

Derk nodded. "That's what I did."

Andrew laughed. "We'll have you carry wood and pick up potatoes, Derk. I'll bet you and the girls could handle that." He winked at the stagecoach driver. Derk's face turned red. He hoped he wouldn't be stuck doing girls' work.

"Give him a chance," Mr. Frink said. "I think Derk will turn out to be a good worker. Give him a chance and he'll prove himself."

+ + + + +

Derk was tired and all his muscles ached. The morning after he arrived at the Wade House, he began work in the sawmill. There was a great demand for lumber in this small settlement. A new inn was to be built, a clapboard house, New England style. It would replace the log cabin that now served as the inn.

All morning Derk skinned bark from round, small tree trunks that would be used as rafters. At noon the workers trooped to the inn for dinner. The smell of hot biscuits tickled Derk's nose and made his stomach growl. He went in and sat down to a bountiful country dinner.

+ + + + +

The first green leaf buds had popped out over the past few days and Derk hoped to get outside and enjoy the sun. He took one last glance through the doors of the blacksmith shop, then turned and gave his full attention to working the bellows. Mr. Wade needed a hot fire to shape the metal into a connecting rod for a wagon.

"Achoo! Achoo!" The sneeze startled Derk. A man wearing wide breeches and a flat cap with a visor stood in the doorway.

"God bless you!" Mr. Wade stopped hammering. "Howdy, I'm Sylvanus Wade. What can I do for you?"

"Wheel broke off my wagon half mile down the road…hit a bad rut. Sent me here. Said you could fix it."

"Derk, you go with him. Hitch the horse to the cart and give him a ride out to his wagon. Help him bring it in." Mr. Wade smiled. "Someday there'll be a plank road to drive on and those ruts will be gone. Won't that be great?"

"Yes. Yes. Thank you most kindly," the man said.

"What are you hauling?" Derk asked as they rode out to the wagon.

"Oh, just some farmer's produce."

"Do you have a farm near here?"

"Usually I haul freight." He took out a tobacco pouch and put a wad into his mouth.

Derk slowed the horse as they neared the wagon.

"Just came to this area…want to set up a freight-hauling business," the man said. "Need someone to help me. Be good money in it for the right person."

"Tell me more," Derk said. "Tell me more."

Chapter 13

A Real Job   Late Summer 1849

It feels like it's time to move on, Derk told himself one morning in late summer. He had been at the Wade House for almost a year. Between the chores and the blacksmith shop, he attended the advanced classes at Mr. Wade's school and completed the courses offered there. The year with the Wade family had been an enjoyable one. The family treated everyone, even those who worked for them, as if they were guests. The food, much of it fresh from the garden, was plentiful and tasty.

Two things were disappointing; Derk still didn't have a diploma and nothing came of the job the freight hauler had promised him. He never saw the man again.

Mr. Wade encouraged him to go to Sheboygan, the county seat. The city was growing; immigrants from Europe arrived almost weekly. Maybe he could find a school there that offered the classes he needed to earn a diploma.

He thanked the Wade family and said good-bye, promising to return and visit them. Later that day he was on his way back to Sheboygan, riding the stage, sitting in the driver's seat next to Mr. Frink.

"Do you have a place to stay in Sheboygan?" Mr. Frink asked. "Do you know someone who lives there?"

Derk shook his head. "I'm hoping someone needs help, maybe at the dock, maybe at a blacksmith shop."

"Where are you going to live?' The stage lurched as they hit a deep rut.

The boy shrugged his shoulders. "I don't know. Maybe someone will hire me and let me stay with them."

"Let me think," the driver said. "Maybe I know someone who could use a young man like you."

After a few minutes, Mr. Frink said, "We have a boarding house...I should say that my wife does, since I'm always driving stagecoach. You could stay with us. My wife's a good cook." He clucked at the horses with his tongue. They sidestepped their way around a fallen tree.

"But...I...I...can't pay you." Derk fumbled for the words." Mr. Wade paid me in room and board. He let me go to school when I wasn't needed for working in the mill or at the blacksmith shop. I'm thankful he gave me a place to live. But I can't pay you."

"But you are willing to work?"

"I'm willing to work. I'll do almost anything to earn some money."

"We could use a strong young man at the boarding house."

Strong? That's the first time anyone has said I'm strong, Derk thought. Mr. Smith had called him "puny" less than two years ago. "I'm willing, but I don't know how strong I am."

"Look at you, Derk. My, you're a foot taller than when I gave you a ride out to Greenbush last fall. And I'll bet you have some good-sized muscles under that jacket."

Derk thought about that. The man was right. He had outgrown his old jacket and Andrew Wade had given him the one he was now wearing. Andrew's old trousers covered Derk's legs down to the tops of his new shoes. He smiled; he had grown; his new clothes were proof.

"That's what blacksmithing does," Mr. Frink said. "It builds muscles. Your friends in Oostburg, what's their name, the Daanes, won't even know you, you've grown so much."

Derk's face broke into a wide grin.

"My wife could use a strong young man to split wood…keep the woodbox full. She can't cook if she doesn't have wood for the fire. Has even more to do now, since the little one came along. Uh, here comes a team and wagon."

Mr. Frink reined in the horses and pulled to the side of the road, allowing the team to pass. The driver raised his hand in greeting as the wagon lumbered past. The wagon box, covered with an old quilt, bulged with boxes. Getting back to the middle of the road meant lurching over the ruts. The horses strained as the stage started again.

"Can you milk cows? I need someone to do the milking. We have a few acres with a barn and some livestock out at the edge of town. You could run errands, tend the garden."

A lone crow cawed from the top branches of a pine tree.

"My wife's always complaining that I'm gone too much, but with this business, you either do it, or you give it up. A stage has to run on a regular schedule. That's another thing you could do – feed and groom the horses when I finish my run for the day."

"I'd be glad to do that," Derk said, "but tell me, is there a school near the boarding house?"

The driver laughed. "Do you always have school on your mind? You must want to be a professor at a university."

"No, I want to be a doctor." Derk surprised himself. Why was he telling this man his dreams?

"A doctor? Why? Was your pa a doctor?"

"No, but he wanted to be. He couldn't get the education he needed, didn't have a chance to go to the university. I don't want that to happen to me."

"I see.... You know, Derk, I'm all for book learning to become a doctor, but there's another way to learn medicine."

Derk frowned. "What do you mean, another way?"

"You could study with a licensed doctor. I have this friend, a doctor, in Sheboygan Falls. He often has a young man studying with him, like an apprentice would. He has an apprentice right now."

Mr. Frink cleared his throat. "They call it 'reading' with the doctor. You would go with the doctor on his house calls, watch how he does things…see what he prescribes. What do you think of that idea?"

Derk took off his cap, smoothed his hair down and put it back on. "I don't know. It doesn't seem right to me, not going to the university to study medicine. They sure do things differently here."

"I don't know how they do things in Holland," the driver said, "but I think it's a good way to learn. Say someone broke a leg. You'd see first-hand how to set it; you can't really learn how to set a broken bone from a book…. Or if someone had a ruptured appendix." Mr. Frink guided the horses around a large rock in the road. "Experience is a big part of becoming a doctor."

He went on. "He's a good man, this doctor in Sheboygan Falls. I have to pick up a package that he's sending to Sheboygan. I'll take you to his home and introduce you."

+ + + + +

Derk took Mr. Frink's offer to stay at the boarding house and work for his keep. He wouldn't be saving for the ticket back home, but this was the best he could do for now.

Mrs. Frink welcomed Derk. Jovial and hardworking, she ran the boarding house with efficiency and hospitality. As her husband said, she was a good cook. Derk enjoyed being with the family, often taking time between chores and studies to play with Jacob, their toddler.

High on a hill, the boarding house overlooked the lake and the waterfront. One day as Derk picked up tree branches in the back yard, he stopped to look at the lake. He saw it. At the dock, sitting in shallow water, was the damaged hull of a ship. It was the *Phoenix*, even though most of what could be salvaged had been removed. He had not seen the remains of the steamer since that awful day.

The sight unnerved him as his mind flooded with memories. He could feel the heat and the smoke filling his lungs and choking him. He could see Ma and Jacobus, black silhouettes against the roaring orange flames, and hear the thunderous sounds from the exploding boiler. He could feel Martin's wet jacket and shivering body. He remembered the despair that overwhelmed him when Mr. Van Doon told him that his family didn't make it.

He began to shake, then slumped to the ground beneath some bushes. After a time, he stood up. It was getting dark. He'd have to hurry to get the chores done before night came.

The Frink's farm on the western edge of town had cows, hogs and chickens. Milking the cows and feeding them and the other livestock became the morning and evening routine. Once a day he cleaned the stalls and put down straw for bedding. Some evenings he was so tired he wanted to fall into bed without studying his lessons for the next day.

One late fall afternoon Derk finished the chores and started back to town carrying two heavy pails of milk. His mind wandered back to Winterswyk and how his sister had to help him carry one pail of milk to the cheese maker. He remembered Pieter's taunt, that Derk needed a girl to help him carry one pail of milk. The thought made him angry. If I ever see Pieter again, he vowed, I'll punch him in the nose.

Derk no longer fit the "scrawny weakling" name that Pieter had called him so long ago. Pieter would be forced to change his mind if he could see Derk's muscles.

And what was Pieter doing? Pieter, no doubt, was attending the university, studying to be a lawyer or a professor. Derk felt himself growing angry at Pieter's good fortune.

And what am I doing? I'm stuck here in Wisconsin, and the most challenging classes that are offered are a review of what I already learned in Greenbush. He wanted to kick at the stone in the road, but he couldn't. He'd spill the milk if he did. True, the classes were forcing him to read and write in English; knowing the language well would always be a plus. He knew that.

Another disappointment for Derk concerned money, or rather his lack of it. Some days he found work at the dock; some days he did odd jobs for the neighbors that paid a few coins.

Looking up, Derk saw a farmer's wagon, bumping through the ruts, coming toward him. The driver stopped the horses when they met. "You live around here?" He gestured with his head toward the town.

Derk set the heavy pails down and nodded.

"Need help unloading. Got a sore back. You're a strong young man."

"I'll have to carry this milk to town first."

"Sure, I'll wait. There'll be a few coins for you."

Derk picked up the pails and set off for town at a quick pace. He carried the pails into the kitchen, thankful that Mrs. Frink wasn't there to give him another job. Slipping out, he softly closed the door behind him.

Stopping at the carriage house at the back of the yard, he grabbed a small lantern off the wall and checked the wick, then the kerosene. Enough to light the way, should he need it.

Twilight was beginning to fade as Derk approached the wagon. The man was slumped on the seat, dozing. The horses neighed.

The man jerked awake and sat up. "Uhhh."

"What's the matter, sir? Are you sick?"

"Uh huh. Back really hurts. Get up here on the wagon." He moved over. "Name's De Haas. Yours?"

"Derk Van Vliet."

They shook hands.

"Got some goods here." He indicated the wagon box with a jerk of his head. "Need to deliver 'em." He clucked his tongue and the horses started. "You're Dutch, aren't you?"

Derk nodded.

"Have family here?"

"I came with my parents some years ago." Derk winced, feeling that familiar twinge of loss. "They were lost in the ship that burned north of here."

"Ach, such tragedy. You really are alone." He shook his head and then was silent for a few minutes. "Could use you in my business... hauling between here and Fond du Lac."

He went on. "Need someone at the dock when settlers come. If they need a wagon to haul their goods to the homestead, I do that. Not everyone can afford a team and wagon, so I help them out."

A short way from town they came to a fork in the road. They turned left. The road was no more than a path which became more and more narrow. The wagon brushed the branches of the trees as they rounded another bend. They came to a small clearing with a log cabin in the center. He stopped the horses at the door.

Derk unloaded the containers from the wagon. After they were stored in the cabin, Mr. De Haas took out a tobacco pouch. "Want a pinch?"

Derk shook his head.

"No tobaccy? Well, I'll have some." Taking a pinch, he put it into his mouth and put the pouch in his pocket. They set out back to town with Derk driving the team.

Time passed and they soon arrived at a building on Third Street, not far from the dock.

De Haas sat on a box and watched as Derk unhitched the horses and led them into their stalls. He wiped them down and gave them water and hay.

"You're good with horses." He spit tobacco juice on the floor in front of him. "Here's a few coins for your work."

Derk stuck them into his pocket. With the lantern lit, he set out for the boarding house, whistling.

De Haas wanted Derk to meet him at the dock whenever a ship with immigrants arrived. With the wagon and team ready to go, Derk would haul the baggage to the building on Third Street and store it there. A day or so later, De Haas would haul their goods to their homestead.

Derk would have to skip school the day the boat came in, but it would be worth it. He finally had a real job.

Chapter 14

Failed Again   June 10, 1850   Morning

Derk tied the team to the hitching post at the dock and climbed the gangplank to the Lake Michigan steamer. The ship was filled with Dutch immigrants, and he hoped many of them needed their baggage transported to their new homesteads.

Most of the time, business had been going reasonably well. Derk met the steamers and hauled the boxes and chests of his customers to the building on Third Street. Then De Haas took over. Since he owned just one team and wagon, De Haas delivered the baggage to the homes.

The men, wearing their wide breeches and visor caps, were up on deck. This was good; the customers were all together in one place.

"Welcome to Sheboygan," Derk said, shaking hands all around. "You'll like it here. How many days did it take to make the trip?"

Most had come from the Netherlands to New York and had taken the Erie Canal or a train across New York State. At Buffalo they had caught the steamer.

"That's how I came, three years ago. Where are you going?"

"Oostburg"…"Gibbsville"… "Cedar Grove."

"You need a place to store your baggage. The hotels in town can put you up, but they don't like to store your chests and boxes for you. I can haul and store them for you. I have a team and wagon tied up right below. I can load your baggage, haul it to a building close by, and when you're ready to go to the homestead, it'll be ready to go, too."

"What do you charge?" a passenger standing near Derk asked.

"Thirty gold coins. You pay fifteen coins when I load it and fifteen when I unload it at your homestead. " Derk took off his visor cap, smoothed his hair down and put the cap back on. "You can save five gold coins if you pay it all when I load your baggage. Then it'll cost you only twenty-five gold coins."

A man whom Derk noticed walked with a limp spoke to the others in Dutch. "I don't trust him. This fellow might be a cheat."

Derk winced. He didn't like this man or what he was doing, trying to persuade others not to hire him. "If you need a wagon to haul your goods, I've got the best price," he said.

Worry began to take over Derk's mind; he needed five or more households to sign up with him to satisfy his boss. Last time a ship had docked, only one family had agreed to buy the hauling service. De Haas had raged at him for what seemed like hours, about how Derk needed to bring in more business, that he couldn't pay him, and on and on. And then De Haas hadn't paid him. Derk had to try again with another pitch. "How are you going to get your household goods out to Cedar Grove? Hire me and I'll get you there in a day."

"How do we know we can trust you?" another man asked.

"You can trust me," Derk said. "I'm a fellow countryman."

"Don't believe him." The man with the limp spoke up "Don't believe him. I've heard that line before. 'Fifteen gold coins to haul your goods and store them so you don't have to worry about them. Fifteen coins when your goods are delivered the next morning. Only twenty-five coins if you pay me right now."

He looked around the group. "I'll tell you what happened to me in New York. I trusted a freight-hauler. Our goods were not delivered to the boat dock the next morning, so I went to the street address. It was an open field. The scoundrel had stolen our goods, and I paid him to steal them!"

No one spoke for a few moments.

"Oh, don't be so hard on him, Schutt," another man said. "He's just a young man, asking for your business."

Schutt? Mr. Schutt from the next farm in Winterswyk? Derk thought. That can't be him...he's not that old...Mr. Schutt didn't walk like that. This man is too old to be our neighbor.

The man they called "Schutt" went on. "I trusted a Dutchman in New York and I lost everything. I had to stay there until I earned enough money to bring my family here." He paused, then turned and pointed out toward the lake. "See that ship's boiler over there? I've been told that's the *Phoenix*, what's left of it. The only good thing about being cheated in New York was that I and my family didn't die in that terrible fire!"

The man turned on his heel and went below. The others followed him. Derk stood, staring after them. Could that man, who looked so much older now, really be the Van Vliet's neighbor? From what he said, he had to be.

The boy wanted to run after Mr. Schutt and tell him he was

Derk from Winterswyk, but he couldn't. He could feel his anger rising. Schutt had ruined all chances of getting any customers, and De Haas would never stop yelling.

Fury welled up as Derk ran down the gangplank, then took off along the beach, running hard. People and dogs scattered as they saw him coming.

Farther on, two small boys were digging in the sand. Derk squashed their buildings with his foot as he charged through. He didn't stop running until he was way, way beyond the town; then he dropped to the sand, exhausted. Putting his head between his knees, he sobbed for a long time.

Why did life have to be so difficult? He'd already endured so much. Leaving his country, his school, his dog…. Losing his family, friends, everything…. Living through the *Phoenix* inferno….. Being alone in a strange land with no next of kin, except a little brother who didn't remember him until he asked him about the wooden rabbit. No one should have to endure that many troubles in a whole lifetime.

True, many folks had been kind to him along the way, he had to admit. The Van Doon family, Mr. Smith, the Daanes, the Wade family, Mr. Frink and his wife, all had been helpful. But he truly was alone. And now, with no customers, customers driven away by an old neighbor, and having to face the De Haas rant….

I've failed again. Derk told himself. Again. Everything that he had tried – everything had turned to ashes, just as the *Phoenix* had. What would he do now?

He thought back to what Mr. Schutt said about the freight-hauler in New York. Derk pictured the scene. He was on the deck of the ship in New York harbor, standing next to his pa. A man dressed in breeches and a flatcap had come on board and told them that he would haul their household goods. The scruffy-bearded man, missing a front tooth, had spit a stream of tobacco juice on the deck, then forced it into the cracks between the boards with the toe of his boot.

Another picture flashed into his mind – the blacksmith shop at the Wade House. As Derk worked the bellows, a man who needed a wagon wheel repaired, ground the tobacco juice into the dirt floor with the toe of his boot.

De Haas had this same habit, spitting tobacco juice and trying to make it disappear into a gravel path, or a barn floor. Or the deck of a ship?

Derk's eyes widened. It couldn't be! Or maybe it was! Scruffy beard, missing tooth, spitting tobacco juice. Was De Haas the same freight-hauler who had stolen Mr. Schutt's household goods in New York? Was he stealing baggage here in Sheboygan? Is that why he wouldn't allow Derk to deliver it to the homesteads? Was he hauling the stuff to Fond du Lac and selling it there? Derk's head was spinning.

"God, what am I going to do?" The words came from his heart in a half-sob. It was a prayer, the first prayer in a long time. Voicing those words aloud seemed to clear his head.

Then he remembered. The horses! He had left them tied to the hitching post at the dock! He jumped up and dashed down the beach, back toward town. What if the horses had broken away? Or someone had stolen the team and wagon?

For a moment Derk dreaded what De Haas would say. The next moment, he realized that it didn't matter what the man said. Derk knew he could no longer work for someone who may have robbed his neighbor.

He would return the team and wagon to the building on Third Street. Then he would run back to the dock to see if he could find Mr. Schutt and convince him that he was Derk Van Vliet from Winterswyk.

Chapter 15

A Family   June 10, 1850   Afternoon

Derk got back to the dock and found the team and wagon just as he had left them. He untied the leather reins and headed toward the building on Third Street, urging the horses into a trot. Chickens scattered and dogs ran along at the wheels, yapping.

Arriving at the building he unhitched the wagon and led the horses inside. De Haas was lying on the bed in the far corner, empty bottle on the floor. He was snoring, effectively drowning out any noises the horses made. Derk walked out and gently closed the door.

He ran to the dock, then stopped to look around at the sea of wagons, horses, baggage and people. He scanned the crowd for the Schutt family. A lady standing near a loaded wagon resembled Mrs. Schutt. She had two small children with her, an infant in her arms and another, hanging unto her skirt, both crying lustily. If this was the Schutt family, Mr. Schutt was nowhere to be seen.

Derk turned to look at the other wagons, fully loaded, leaving the dock, but did not see Mr. Schutt, or anyone who looked like the man he had seen that morning on the steamer. Was he too late?

Glancing back at what he thought might be the Schutt family, he saw a man stand up at the far side of the wagon, then walk, limping, around to the back. He looked like the man on the steamer who had been called "Schutt" that morning. Derk forced himself to walk toward the wagon, wondering what he would say when he got there. "Dear Lord, please help."

"Good afternoon, Mr. Schutt," Derk said.

The man stared at him blankly.

Derk continued. "I think we met this morning, on the deck of the steamer. I didn't recognize you at first, but when someone called you 'Schutt,' I thought maybe you were our neighbor from Winterswyk."

The man peered closely at Derk. "Who are you?"

"I'm Derk Van Vliet, from Winterswyk, from the next farm."

"No. You're the Van Vliet's son? Derk? Little Derk?" He took out a handkerchief and blew his nose. "I never would have known you. You've changed so much! We never heard...I thought your whole family...the ship...the fire...."

"Not Martin and me. We were in a lifeboat that got to shore. The others were in a lifeboat, too, but it tipped over."

"I'm sorry, Derk." Mr. Schutt gave him an awkward hug, then reached for his handkerchief again. "Hannah! Hannah! Look who's here!" he shouted to be heard over the crying children. They walked to the front of the wagon. "This is our old neighbor from Winterswyk, Derk!"

Mrs. Schutt gave a cry. "Derk? Derk! We thought...your family...I'm so sorry for you." She put her hand on his arm and slowly shook her head. "You've been through so much. I'm so sorry." She put the crying baby on her shoulder and patted it on the back.

"Derk, I can't believe it's really you! You're so grown up," Mr. Schutt said. "And you say Martin was rescued, too?"

"Yes, Martin and me. He's living with the family that first took us in, the Van Doons.

"Martin…I bet he's changed a lot, too. He was just a toddler when we saw him last," Mrs. Schutt said, patting the baby. "I still can't believe it's you, Derk. You're almost as tall as your pa. You know, your ma used to worry about how puny you were. She didn't need to worry…that's for sure!"

She rocked the baby back and forth in her arms. "Shush, little one. You'll have to excuse me. This child is having a terrible time today. I think I'll try to feed her."

Mr. Schutt climbed onto the wagon and arranged a place for his wife to sit. Then he helped her and the other child unto the wagon.

"Come, Derk, look at this." Schutt walked to the back of the wagon. "I bought this wagon this morning, and it seems like this wheel isn't quite right. Look at it. What do you think?" He squatted and pointed to the place where the wheel joined the axle.

Derk squatted beside him and looked at the wheel.

Suddenly Schutt turned to Derk and said, "Derk, you were at the steamer this morning. You had the wagon for hire."

The young man nodded.

"When I spoke against freight-haulers this morning, I didn't know I was turning away your customers. I'm sorry."

"That's all right. I just quit my job with the man who owns the team and wagon. You know the man who cheated you in New York? I think he's the same man I've been working for here."

"What?" Schutt lost his balance and fell backward on the sand. "What? What did you say?"

Derk stood up, held out his hand and helped Schutt up. "I think he's the same man who cheated you in New York."

"You think that man is here in town? You've been working for him? What did he hire you to do?"

"Just what I was doing this morning…go to the dock and get customers whenever immigrants come in, then haul their goods to his building in town. I didn't suspect he was stealing until earlier today. Now I'm quite sure of it."

"You haven't done any other work for him?"

Derk shook his head. "No, that's all he'd let me do, although I begged him for more work."

"Why do you think he's the same man?"

"It's hard to say, but so many things add up."

"Like what?"

Derk went through the list, starting with the missing tooth, the tobacco spitting, the similar salesman pitch he had used in New York. "And I just thought of something else. I helped him unload a wagon full of chests and boxes at a cabin in the woods, not too far from here. That was the first time I worked for him. That's the only other thing I've done for him."

Schutt took off his cap, rubbed his forehead and then replaced the cap.

"I didn't pay much attention to it then," Derk said, "but the

115

chests were tagged like ours were when we got on the ship in Holland. They were tagged with Dutch names. And, he refused to let me deliver any baggage to a new homestead, even when it went to Gibbsville and I could have visited Martin."

"I'm glad you're not involved any more than you already are," Mr. Schutt said. He walked to the front of the wagon. "Hannah, where is that 'Wanted' flyer?"

"It's packed with our Bible, in there." She pointed to a large bag. "Why do you want that?"

"I want to show it to Derk." He turned to Derk. "These flyers were given out at the time a Dutch immigrant family was murdered in New York City. I don't know if the man did that, but I think this is the man who cheated us."

Derk looked at the flyer and gasped. "That's him…still looks the same…missing tooth…beard…De Haas – he didn't even change his name!"

Mr. Schutt looked at his wife. "Do you think you and the children can stay here in the wagon for a while longer? Derk and I are going to the sheriff."

"The sheriff?" Derk asked. "Why?"

"De Haas is wanted for murder in New York State. We'll turn him in to the authorities."

The sheriff and two deputies followed Mr. Schutt and Derk to the Third Street building. The officers went in; De Haas was there, sleeping. They asked Mr. Schutt to step inside with them to identify the man.

"He's the man," the officer said to Derk when they came out. "The deputies will arrest him and lock him up."

Mr. Schutt went back to his family at the waterfront and Derk and the sheriff walked back to his office.

"We've had complaints from immigrants having their property stolen," the sheriff said. "Can you show me the way to the cabin?"

"Yes, I can."

The cabin was filled with the evidence, boxes and chests, all bearing Dutch names. The officer made a list of names on the containers. They got back on the horses and rode to town.

"I'll match this list of names with the list of those reporting missing goods. If they match, we've got our man."

"What happens if De Haas finds out I helped turn him in?"

"I don't think you need to worry. Do you know of anyone else who worked for him?"

"No, I don't."

"Don't worry. He'll be in jail until we can prove that he stole from the immigrants; then we'll send him to New York on these murder charges. He'll never come back to Wisconsin."

+ + + + +

It had been a long day and Derk was weary and hungry. The farm chores were done and it felt good to be sitting with the Schutts, enjoying Mrs. Frink's chicken dinner at the boarding house.

Later Mr. Schutt and Derk sat on the porch. A gentle evening breeze ruffled Derk's hair.

"I need help building a cabin and clearing land," Mr. Schutt began. "Hannah and I would like you to help us. In turn, we'd give you a home, be part of our family. We'd like to have Martin live with us, too, if that could be worked out. How does that sound to you?"

"The 'home' part and seeing more of Martin sounds wonderful," Derk said. "But I'm too tired to do any more thinking today. Before I say yes, I want to think it through again."

"I don't need an answer right now," Mr. Schutt said. "But whether you say yes or no, I would like you to go with me tomorrow to see some farm land at Gibbsville. I want to look at it before I buy it."

"Gibbsville? I haven't seen Martin in a long time. Can we stop to see him?"

"I think that would work." He stroked his beard. "Yes, we'll stop to see him."

Will Martin know who I am? Derk wondered. Will he remember me? He stretched. "I should be going to bed, but I want to thank you for what you did to put De Haas behind bars."

"And I'm glad that De Haas will finally pay the price for all the wrong he's done," Mr. Schutt said. He took a deep breath. "Derk, I'm so thankful that you came looking for me, even after I made you lose customers this morning."

"It was all for the best, Mr. Schutt. It was all for the best."

"Your parents would be so proud of you, Derk. I hope I can do

118

as well raising my little ones. You're not afraid of hard work, you're trying to get an education, you have goals and plans, even after all you've been through. Yes, I know your parents would be proud of you."

Derk watched the fireflies appear and disappear as their lights blinked on and off in the darkness. "One thing has been missing," Derk said, "and I know my parents wouldn't like it. Sunday worship has been occasional, at best."

"It's been occasional for us, too," the man said, "but I hope to change that as soon as we've built our cabin. I want to invite the neighbors to worship with us, just like we did back in Winterswyk."

"Yes, but without the officials watching."

"Amen to that!" Mr. Schutt said. "Amen to that!"

Chapter 16

A Home   June 11, 1850

"Ma, guess who stopped in to see us," Peter said as he and Derk walked into the cabin.

"Hello, Mrs. Daane."

She turned from the pot of soup she was stirring over the fire. "Ooh, it's Derk! It's good to see you again." Putting the spoon on the table next to the bread trough, she grasped Derk's upper arms with her hands and looked up at him. "My, I can't believe how much you've grown! You're so tall, I have to look up to you now." She gave his arms a squeeze. "And those muscles!"

Derk smiled. "I guess that's what hard work does for you."

"What brings you to Oostburg today?"

"I'm on my way to see some land near Gibbsville with Mr. Schutt. He and his wife were friends of my parents back in Winterswyk, and they just arrived in Sheboygan. They've asked me to help build a cabin and live with them."

Mrs. Daane smiled. "Why, that's wonderful! Are you going to do it?"

"It's a great offer, but I'm still thinking about it. They want Martin to come and live there, too, if that works out."

"I'm so surprised to see you that I'm forgetting my manners." She pulled out a chair for him. "Please sit down."

"I'd like to, but I can't. Mr. Schutt is waiting for me and we want to stop to see Martin. So I should go, although I'd like to stay. Good to see you."

Mrs. Daane smiled. "You're welcome here, anytime, Derk. Be sure you come see us again."

The boys walked out to the horses. Mr. Schutt was in the saddle, talking with Mr. Daane.

"Are you still talking in your sleep, Derk?" Peter asked the question as Derk mounted his horse.

Derk shrugged his shoulders. "I was afraid you'd say something about that. I've been thinking about what your pa said, but I'm still puzzling over the two people in prison cells."

"You mean who the two people are? You'll figure it out, Derk. It'll become obvious." He paused. "Thanks for stopping. Hope everything works out well for the new homestead."

"Ready to go?" Mr. Schutt asked.

They said good-bye and picked up the trail toward Gibbsville.

The young man looked up at the sky. Crows cawed to each other as they flew among the treetops. Green leaves in full bloom stood out against the white puffy clouds filling the June sky.

Derk's thoughts drifted toward Peter's question. Why did Peter have to remind him about his problem with Pieter in Winterswyk? Derk usually tried to put that conflict out of his mind; he always felt his anger rising when he thought about how Pieter had destroyed their "best friend" relationship so many years ago. It was no different today; he could feel himself getting angry at his old enemy. One prison cell was for Pieter, but the second one, who was locked in that cell?

Mr. Schutt interrupted his thoughts. "Same skies here as in Holland. Wisconsin sure is beautiful in June."

Derk agreed.

At the Van Doon homestead Derk introduced Mr. Schutt to the family, then went to look for Martin. He found him near the garden, playing with the younger Van Doon children.

"Hello, Martin. I'm your brother. Do you remember me?"

The child shrugged his shoulders.

"Do you have a toy rabbit?"

Martin smiled and reached into his pocket. He brought the rabbit out and gave it to Derk. The lines Derk had carved inside the ear were nearly rubbed out, worn smooth by Martin's hands.

"Who made this rabbit for you?"

"You did."

Derk gave the rabbit back to him. "Put this in your pocket and don't lose it," he said, tousling his brother's hair.

"I won't Derk. I'll keep it forever."

Derk squatted and looked his brother straight in the eyes. "Martin, maybe I'll live on a farm, close by, if Mr. Schutt buys the land. Maybe we'll get to see each other every day. Would you like that?"

"Yes."

Jumping to his feet, Derk took the child by his arms and swung him around, feet flying out behind him. He put him down.

Martin shook with laughter. "Do it again," he begged. "Do it again!"

"Do you remember the piggyback rides I gave you a long time ago?"

"No."

"No? I'll have to make up for lost time and give you one right now." Bending down, Derk helped Martin scramble up on his back. Around the farmyard they went together until it was time for Derk to leave with Mr. Schutt.

"Take me with you, Derk," Martin said as he slid off his brother's back. "I want to come and live with you. Then you can swing me around everyday."

"I'd like to have you live with me, too," Derk said, "but I have to find a home for us first. I see Mr. Schutt is ready to go. Maybe I can come to see you more often. Would you like that?"

"Yes, but I want to live with you."

"We'll have to wait and see," Derk said as he got on his horse. He turned and waved at his brother as they rode west.

"Good people, the Van Doons," Mr. Schutt said, after they were on their way.

"They sure are," Derk said. "They took us in, gave us a home. If they hadn't, I don't know where we'd be today." A squirrel high in an oak tree chattered as they passed by.

"And the Daanes, too," Derk went on. "They are wonderful. Living with them that first summer, when I had no other place to go…. And Peter's friendship helped me through that first awful year. And he's still a good friend."

The man smiled. "The Daanes and the Van Doons – when our cabin's done and we have worship services, we'll invite them."

He went on. "Mr. Van Doon told me about the property we'll be looking at. It touches their land and has a river flowing through the back acres. I think he called it the Onion River. Wonder how it got that name."

"That's a funny name for a river."

"I've got some good news," Mr. Schutt said. "The Van Doons offered to let us live in their second cabin while we build ours. Now we won't have to build a lean-to; that'll save time. We can start with the cabin right away."

"That will be so much easier on your wife and the girls," Derk said, "and on us, too. With a roof over our heads and a bed to sleep in every night, building the cabin should go quickly."

The property was covered with oak and maple trees. White-tailed deer, hiding in a thicket, bounded away. The horses ambled through the trees to the far side of the tract. At the top of a small knoll they stopped. Below them lay the river.

"What do you think, Derk?" Mr. Schutt asked, after a long time of gazing at the tranquil scene.

"I like it. It's beautiful land with rich soil. You should have seen the vegetables Mrs. Daane grew, big cabbages, onions, corn." He gestured toward the river. "And it's good to have a river for watering the livestock. All around, it looks good to me."

"Looks good to me, too," Mr. Schutt said. "I think we've found ourselves some land of our own."

Chapter 17

A Country June 12, 1850

Derk didn't awaken until the sunlight was streaming into the window. He bolted out of bed and dressed. Racing to the kitchen, he grabbed the milk pails on his way out the door.

This may be the last day I'll be doing chores for the Frinks, Derk thought. He had told Mr. and Mrs. Frink about Mr. Schutt's offer. They said he could stay on with them, find another job, and maybe the new academy that was to be built would be a place to get a diploma. Whatever his choice, the Frink's wished him well.

Derk had some serious thinking to do; he had to give Mr. Schutt his answer tonight. Should he go with the Schutts and be part of their family? Martin would like that.

He placed the stool next to the cow and sat down, pressing his head against the cow's warm side. The milk started to fill the pail. In memory, Derk was back in Winterswyk, milking the goat. So much had happened since then. The Netherlands seemed almost a lifetime away.

The university at Leyden…did he want to study medicine there? Should he "read" with the doctor in Sheboygan Falls? Would he regret it later if he didn't go to the university?

Family? If he went to Holland, would Martin stay in America? It would be difficult now to leave Martin behind.

Bello... Elizabeth? Three years had passed. Why hadn't she answered his letter?

His thoughts chased themselves around his mind, "just like Bello chasing his tail," Derk said aloud. "A dog chasing his tail never gets anywhere, and that's what I'm doing. I don't know if I can trust myself to make the right decision." He finished feeding the animals and started back to town with the pails of milk.

After breakfast, Derk got the shovel and rake from the carriage house and turned over the soil in the garden. He raked it smooth; Mrs. Frink could plant the garden today.

Derk ate quickly, barely tasting the beef roast, potatoes and carrots. He wanted to go back to the beach and sort through his thoughts. "Lord, I need help to make the correct decision," he said aloud.

He walked to the dock and glanced at the boiler of the *Phoenix*, ready for the wave of emotions to wash over him. He felt a twinge of sadness. That's another way I've grown, he thought. It's not that I don't feel sad about my family, but what happened that day no longer controls my life. He walked along the edge of the water, found a stick, and threw it in. The waves brought the stick back to shore and dumped it at his feet.

He turned northward, thinking about the blinding rage that sent him running up the beach earlier that week. How could I be so angry that I would knock down those buildings in the sand, he wondered. Those little boys…they're about Martin's age. I wouldn't want anything like that to happen to him. How can I make it right? I can tell them I'm sorry and ask for their forgiveness…. If I find them, I'll tell them I'm sorry. He stopped, sat down and took off his clogs and socks. He dug his feet deep into the sand, feeling the damp coolness.

His mind wandered to Pa's words the night he had overheard his parents talking about coming to America. "Derk should have the chance I didn't have." Derk remembered Pa saying that as clearly as if it had been yesterday. Would he get the education that his parents wanted for him?

Far up the beach he could see two small boys digging in the sand. Maybe it was them…but maybe they'd be very angry. Maybe I shouldn't apologize…just leave things as they are. Pulling his feet out, he rubbed the sand off with his socks, and put on his shoes. He walked slowly up the beach.

He walked toward the boys, then stopped, wondering if they'd recognize him. Maybe they'd run when they saw him coming. Derk walked closer and squatted down so he could talk with them.

"What are you building?" he asked.

They looked at him with odd expressions, but didn't answer.

Derk tried again, this time in Dutch.

"A house," the older one answered. He went back to digging.

"Did you see a boy, about as tall as me, come running through here a few days ago?"

"Yes, a big boy ran through here…knocked our buildings down."

"He was going so fast," the smaller boy added. "He almost knocked us down."

"I'm sorry that happened," Derk said. "I'm the boy who did that, but I'm sorry that I did."

They looked at him, their eyes wide. "Why did you come back? Are you going to knock our buildings down again?"

"No, no, no. I came to say I'm sorry. I'm sorry I knocked your buildings down. Will you forgive me?"

"I guess so, but don't ever do it again," the older one said. "Promise you'll never do it again?"

"I promise."

The boys went back to digging. It seemed the conversation was over; Derk stood up to leave.

The older child spoke. "Our cousin...she saw the whole thing." He lifted up a shovel of dry sand, held it at an angle, and let the sand run slowly off the shovel. "She was very mad at you, very, very mad."

"Oh. Who's your cousin?"

"Elizabeth. She came on a boat. She watches us, from up on the hill. Do you want to tell her you're sorry?"

Derk hesitated. "Well...uh."

"We weren't so mad at you, but Elizabeth was...you should tell *her* you're sorry."

"Well...uh." He had walked into a trap of his own making. "I... I guess I could do that."

"Elizabeth!" The older child shouted. "Come here! Please."

Derk turned and looked toward the hill. A girl about his age stood up and walked slowly down the hill toward them.

"Here's the big boy who knocked our buildings down," the older child said. "Are you going to give him a tongue-lashing now? You said you would if you ever saw him again." The girl's cheeks turned crimson.

Derk took off his cap. "I ran through here a few days ago and knocked their buildings down. I uh…I came to tell the boys that I was sorry. I'm really sorry." He paused. "I…I'm ready for the tongue-lashing."

She blushed again. "Oh, I didn't really mean it," she protested quietly. Then she said in a firm voice, "But you should be more careful. I saw you run through here, and you were going like someone possessed."

"Yes, Miss. I was angry, awfully angry, but you're right, I should be more careful. I'll be more careful from now on."

"I just arrived on the steamer," she said, "and when I saw you destroy the boys' buildings, I thought people here didn't care about children. I told Pieter I wanted to get on the boat and go back to Winterswyk!"

"You're from Winterswyk?"

"Yes. We're staying with Pa's uncle; he lives right up there." She turned and pointed up the hill.

Derk's thoughts raced. Pieter? Elizabeth? "Did you live across the street from the cheese maker?"

"Why, yes. How do you know where I lived?"

"Did someone give you a dog named Bello?"

Her eyes widened and her jaw dropped. "Derk?"

130

He clutched his cap with both hands and nodded. For a moment both stood there and stared. Then both talked at once.

"I was hoping I'd find...."

"You've changed so...."

They laughed.

"Let's start over," Derk said. "Would you like to sit down?" He led the way to an old log lying on the sand.

"I can't believe my eyes. You've changed so much, Derk. I wouldn't have known you."

He nodded. "And I wouldn't have known you." He took a deep breath. "So you just came on the steamer. Did your Pa and Ma come, too?"

"Yes."

"I'm surprised that your family left Holland. Your pa had a good business...he was the only wheel maker in town. Why did you come?"

"You might say we were forced to leave. After you left, more changes came in the church. Pa lost customers because he spoke out against the changes. Then he wasn't able to pay his bills or the taxes and he lost the business." She brushed at the blonde ringlets that framed her face.

Derk stared at the sand and slowly shook his head. "That's terrible. That's so unfair."

"That was bad, but then the church took away his eldership because he wasn't as rich as the other elders. You lose your business, you're lower class," she snapped her fingers, "just like that."

"That's so wrong."

"They called us dompers and threw mud at us, all over our clothes. It was so awful. Ma's condition worsened after Pa lost his business. Pa's uncle said we should come to America and start over. He came to Winterswyk on business and paid for our passage on the ship."

Dompers! Derk thought about how much that word had hurt him when Pieter called him that name. Now Pieter knew how it felt.

"Pieter…did he come?"

"Yes. He dropped out of school, no money for tuition. It was a terrible time…but we're glad to be here." She flicked a leaf off her skirt. "What about you? Where are you living? And why were you so angry that you knocked the boys' buildings down?"

"I was so angry about…that's a long story and I'll tell you later, I promise." He raised his hand as if he were in court, swearing to tell the truth. "I'm staying at a boarding house. Do you remember the Schutt family from Winterswyk?"

"Yes, we came together on the steamer from Buffalo."

"They asked me to help them homestead and want me to live with them. I have to decide today if I'll go with them, or stay in Sheboygan. I came down to the lake to sort through my thoughts and try to decide what I should do."

"Elizabeth!"

They turned to see a young man standing at the top of the hill.

"Pieter! It's Derk!" She cupped her hands around her mouth. "IT'S DERK!"

Standing up abruptly, Derk looked up the hill and turned to walk away.

"Derk! Wait! Derk!"

Derk broke into a run, knowing he could outrun Pieter. A short distance down the beach, Derk lost his footing and stumbled. His shoe came off and as he snatched it from the sand, Pieter grabbed his arm and held on.

"Derk, I just want to talk to you. Are you still mad about being called a domper? That happened a long time ago. You can't be angry about that any longer."

Wrenching his arm free, Derk shouted, "I should punch you in the nose for saying that. Don't tell me how long I can be angry! I thought you were my friend, and when I needed a friend the most, you betrayed me!" The venom that had been stored for so long came spilling out.

He caught his breath, then went on. "You don't know how awful it is to have your pa in jail, be forced to drop out of school, and have your friend call you a stupid fool!"

Pieter stood silent, staring at him.

"You don't know what it's like to lose your family, your friend, and your dog."

Pieter stuck one foot out in front of him and moved the sole of his shoe over the sand again and again, smoothing it over. "I'm really sorry about all you went through, Derk," he said at last. "I had no idea the hurt was so deep. All those things…those difficult things you had to face…and alone…you had to face them alone. Any one of those things by itself is a heavy load to carry. I'm sorry."

"What happened to our 'best friends forever' promise? You didn't keep your part!"

"I see now how badly I treated you," Pieter said. "I didn't keep my promise. I did fail you. Will you forgive me? Can we be friends again?"

Derk realized he was holding his shoe. He dumped out the sand from it and sat down. Taking off the other shoe, he dumped the sand, then put them on.

Pieter spoke. "I don't want there to be a wall between us, Derk. Will you forgive me?"

Should I forgive Pieter for what he did to me? Derk asked himself. No! I have a right to be mad at him forever! Look at what he did to me! As he sat there, he found he was getting angry, just thinking about it.

And then he understood. The two prison cells that Mr. Daane had spoken about became clear: one cell was for Pieter, because he, Derk, wouldn't forgive Pieter. He had put Pieter in prison, locking him out of his life.

And he knew whom the second prison cell was for. It was for… himself. The second cell was for himself, because he, Derk, had locked himself in the prison of anger. Every time he had thought about Pieter in the past few years, he had become angry, extremely angry all over again.

Derk had a choice. Should he forgive, or stay angry?

Pieter spoke again. "I don't want this problem to stand between us. Can we be friends again?"

You've held a grudge against Pieter long enough, Derk told himself. He stood up.

"A friend told me that when I hold a grudge, I put two people in prison cells. I always knew that one cell was for you, Pieter. I just realized that the other cell was for me. I want out of that prison cell! I forgive you, Pieter." Derk held out his hand. "Shake?"

"I'm not sure what you mean about two prison cells," Pieter said. "But I understand you when you say, 'I forgive you.'" He held out his hand.

They shook hands and Derk felt all the bitterness and anger in his heart drain away. He felt free again.

"I'll explain the prison cells sometime," Derk said, looking back toward the boys and Elizabeth. "Now I want to ask your sister about Bello."

"Sure."

As they tramped up the beach toward the others, Derk said, "You dropped out of the university, Pieter. Are you planning to go back?" They reached the log and Derk sat down.

Pieter shrugged his shoulders, then sat down beside his sister. "I don't know. What about your dream of becoming a doctor? Do you want to go to Holland and study at the university someday?"

At that instant, Derk knew what he would do. Everything he needed...wanted...was here in America...a home...a family that included his little brother...and a chance to study medicine...all here, in this new country, his country. He would go with the Schutts, help them homestead, and when Mr. Schutt no longer needed his help, he'd "read" with the doctor in Sheboygan Falls.

"There's a doctor in the next town who takes young men as apprentices," Derk said. "They call it 'reading' with the doctor. I'd learn how to be a doctor by watching him, going on house calls, checking on patients. Later on I'd take care of patients under his supervision."

"They certainly do things differently in America," Pieter said. "Do you think that's wise, learning to be a doctor just by watching someone?"

"I've always thought university training was the best way," Derk said. "That's why I was so determined to go back to Holland. But I can get experience working with this doctor. I'll be learning by doing."

"This is America," Elizabeth said. "So what if Holland does it differently. I think that helping a doctor is a good way to learn."

The sound of waves washing up on shore filled the momentary silence.

Derk took a deep breath and asked, "Elizabeth, how did you and Bello get along?"

She gave a cry and jumped up. "I almost forgot!" Golden braids streaming out behind her, she raced up the hill.

Derk watched her disappear, then shook his head. What's wrong, he wondered.

"Where are you living, Derk?" Pieter asked.

"At a boarding house here in town. I help out with the chores, but today is my last day there."

"Your last day? What are you going to do tomorrow?"

"The Schutts asked me to help them homestead. I'll help with building a cabin and clearing land for crops. I leave with them tomorrow."

Elizabeth appeared at the top of the hill. She carried a basket as she walked carefully down the slope. "Pieter, Pa needs your help now."

Pieter clapped Derk on the back. "I have to go, Derk. When will I see you again? Let's go fishing sometime this summer."

"That would be great, Pieter...after the cabin is built."

Pieter whistled as he climbed the hill.

"This is for you, Derk," Elizabeth said as she handed him the basket. A blanket covered the top.

"What's this?" Derk asked.

The two boys, shovels in hand, stood up, smiled at each other, and crowded around Elizabeth and Derk.

"I'll show you." She folded back the blanket and brought out a small, round bundle of fur.

Derk gasped.

A pink tongue licked Elizabeth's hand. "Bello couldn't come, but one of her puppies could."

The puppy had the same markings and rich, deep coloring as Bello.

Derk wiped his eyes with the back of his hand.

"It's so soft and furry," the younger child said, stroking the puppy's head.

Elizabeth held the puppy out to Derk. "You can hold him."

Derk took the puppy and it nestled into the crook of his arm. "What's its name?"

"I'm waiting for you to name him, since it's your puppy."

Derk shook his head in disbelief. "Elizabeth, I don't know how you did this! How did you manage to bring...all I can say is thank you, thank you, thank you!"

"I had help." She raised her eyes toward the sky.

Derk looked up, too. The sun was sinking. "Oh, no! I have chores to do. I...I can't take the puppy with me now. There's no good place to keep him. After the cabin's built, I'll have a place. Will you keep him for me, until I can take him to the homestead?"

"Sure."

Derk held the puppy out to her and she took it. "Thank you, Elizabeth. I'll be back...soon."

"We'll be here." She turned to her cousins. "Boys, it's time to pick up the shovels and go home." She put the puppy into the basket.

Before she folded the blanket over the sleeping pup, Derk

stroked its soft head again.

He watched as the three trudged up the hill. At the top, Eliza-beth, with the basket on her arm and silhouetted against the sun, turned and waved, then disappeared.

Derk waved and then took off down the beach, running – whooping and hollering inside.

About the Author

When Mary Jane Gruett moved to Sheboygan County, the tragic story of the fire which doomed the Great Lakes steamer, the *Phoenix*, intrigued her. While doing research, she met descendants of *Phoenix* survivors who were eager to have their story remembered. She thought this piece of Wisconsin history, largely unknown, should be retold. The groundwork was in place; the *Shadow of the Phoenix* could be built on that foundation.

When the author was not working on the *Phoenix* story the last fifteen years, she was teaching, tutoring, gardening and writing stories for children. She enjoys spending time with her grandchildren and biking through the Wisconsin country side with her husband.

About the Artist

Jenna De Troye is a self-taught artist who desires to create realistic works that display the beauty of God's creation. Jenna's parents noticed her talent in art at a young age. While they home schooled their daughter they strongly encouraged and supported her endeavors in art throughout the years.

Jenna most enjoys working with pen and ink and pencil and watercolor mediums. Her goal is to capture the viewer's mind and draw them into the depths of art and imagination.

Original artwork by Jenna appears on pages four, thirty-six and seventy-four.

Shadow of the Phoenix

Shadow of the Phoenix

Shadow of the Phoenix

Shadow of the Phoenix

Made in the USA
Charleston, SC
15 July 2013